The Running Boy and Other Stories

The Running Boy and Other Stories

By Megumu Sagisawa

Translated with an Introduction by
Tyran Grillo

CORNELL EAST ASIA SERIES
An Imprint of
Cornell University Press
Ithaca and London

Series: New Japanese Horizons
Series Editors: Michiko N. Wilson / Gustav Heldt / Doug Merwin

First published 2020 by Cornell University Press

Library of Congress Cataloging-in-Publication Data

Names: Sagisawa, Megumu, 196—2004, author. | Grillo, Tyran, translator, writer
    of introduction.
Title: The running boy and other stories / by Megumu Sagisawa ; translated with
    an introduction by Tyran Grillo
Other titles: Kakeru shōnen. English
Description: Ithaca [New York] : Cornell University Press, 2020. |
    Series: Cornell East Asia series no. 201 |
Identifiers: LCCN 2019052591 (print) | LCCN 2019052592 (ebook) |
    ISBN 9781501749889 (paperback) | ISBN 9781501749896 (epub) |
    ISBN 9781501749902 (pdf)
Subjects: LCSH: Short stories, Japanese—20th century—Translations into English.
Classification: LCC PL861.A4267 K3513 2020 (print) | LCC PL861.A4267 (ebook) |
    DDC 895.63/5—dc23
LC record available at https://lccn.loc.gov/2019052591
LC ebook record available at https://lccn.loc.gov/2019052592

Cover: Photographs used with permissions from Sunyoung Yim (*front:* "Running
Boy") and Alao Yokogi (*back:* photograph of Megumu Sagisawa).

Number 201 in the Cornell East Asia Series

Contents

The Running Boy and Other Stories

Running on Water

A TRANSLATOR'S INTRODUCTION

Tyran Grillo

> Confronted with the reality that we understand noth-
> ing and are in over our heads, it's all we can do to run
> the other way.
>
> *Diary entry of Megumu Sagisawa, July 5, 2000*

Megumu Sagisawa was born Megumi Matsuo, the youngest of four girls, on June 20, 1968, in Tokyo. At nineteen, she became the youngest author to win the Bungakukai Prize for new authors for her novel *The Path by the River* (*Kawaberi no michi*, 1987). Two years later her follow-up, *The Deceased* (*Kaerenu hitobito*, 1989), was nominated for the prestigious Akutagawa Prize. Her work has been translated into Italian and Korean, and here for the first time into English. In addition to being a prolific fiction writer, she was a noted essayist and a translator of children's picture books. At twenty-two, she married film director Gō Rijū, only to divorce him a year later. She drove a stick shift, was known to play a mean game of mah-jongg, and could drink anyone under the table. The contrast between her sleek exterior and hardened interior fed her writing with the experiential authenticity of someone twice her age. Sagisawa's oeuvre thus provokes awareness of inevitable discomforts. Her philosophy is built not around the realization that life is pointless but that too many of us spend it without questioning what came before (our histories), what lies ahead (our ambitions), and what remains hidden within (our identities).

The Running Boy (*Kakeru shōnen*, 1992) is quintessential Sagisawa. Written in 1989, this three-part collection won her the Izumi Kyōka Prize for Literature, not least for its unflinching insight into the human condition. With grace and a touch of uncertainty, she paints a monochromatic world, punctuated occasionally with bursts of color. Through it all runs a current of renunciation, offering glimpses of a transcendent future in a society that has yet to bury the bodies from its past. *The Running Boy* is not therapy, but is therapeutic; not catharsis, but nevertheless cathartic.

Her characters grapple with notions of personal versus absolute identity, patiently working themselves into states of reflection while digging into familial and platonic relationships in the shadows of childhood uncertainties. Fantasy takes briefest flight in *The Running Boy*, and when it does appear serves as a mechanism of entrenchment rather than escape. After all, Sagisawa is less interested in showing us the sky than in steeping us in the mud below it. In doing so, she gives an honest, if tainted, lens through which to view the world and ourselves in it. None of the book's stories embody these precepts more solemnly than the opening "Galactic City" ("Ginga no machi"), which centers on a run-down snack bar and its dwindling cadre of loyal customers. The youngest of them, Tatsuo, sees in the oldest of them what he will become one day.

The story opens at the bar in question. Dark and stained with time, the Koyuki is crumbling host to frayed memories. It doesn't merely shelter depravity of habit but embodies it to the fullest. On the inside, it feels almost too familiar. There are many like it in the world, and its uniqueness comes through in the regulars who haunt it. Even they seem to be just fixtures in the bar's dilapidated decor. Most conversations there recycle the past as if to resuscitate a patient who insists on dying. In this sense, the Koyuki is a repository of lost days and perhaps better times. It is pregnant with the vibrancy and idealism of youth, yet births only threadbare nostalgia. Even the curtain in the doorway, caked with decades of fumes and intoxication, is a barrier to a far crueler world.

But just what lies outside the Koyuki's walls? Is it an insurmountable cesspool of lies and corruption or something less dramatic? From Tatsuo's point of view, society abides by its own rhythms. A nearby expressway looms like progress incarnate, sprawling with a network of ramps and traffic. If those roads are the veins of an organism whose heart is the city, then the Koyuki is the kidney filtering the muck of human dross, an underappreciated yet vital organ for the functioning of the whole. Which is to say that those for whom it is a second home are "less than" only because in a social landscape charted by "more thans" they are nonentities, bottom-feeders whose labor outweighs individuality.

Tatsuo is physically affected by his surroundings. His apartment is cold and unforgiving. Its interior glows red from an emergency exit sign outside his window: a potent symbol externalizing his misgivings while bleeding possibilities he will never have the fortitude to pursue. There is no clear exit for him. On the streets, he staggers on drunken legs, navigating potholes and darkness with a vague sense of purpose. In a rare poetic moment, the city is characterized as a "light trap." Alluring and seductive, it is a harbinger of self-destruction, and we sense that Tatsuo is almost glad he hit the eject button when he did, even if the circumstances leading to his exile from the corporate sector were less than ideal. This touching evocation of galactic imagery may be indicative of mystical forces at work, telling Tatsuo that in the end, his mistakes amount to a blink of the cosmic eye.

The opening dream sequence of the title story shifts vantage points. After scouring hidden recesses of a nocturnal city, we find ourselves high above it all, enveloped by gentle ocean breezes and the sweltering heat of a bright summer's day. A boy struggles to stay above water as he runs across a row of planks bobbing on its surface, knowing his fears will pull him under. When the dreamer, Tatsushi, makes his first efforts to locate a lost relative, he holds only snatches of memory as the compass rose for a journey of self-discovery.

On the surface, Tatsushi would seem to be the polar opposite of Tatsuo, even as he is reflective of Sagisawa herself, who in real life had a father with two names and found secrets lurking in a family register. After ferreting out those secrets, Tatsushi learns just how deeply he has relied on a past of his own making to shape who he is in the present. His entrepreneurial tendencies seem an extension of the dreams his father never fulfilled. He recognizes his father's sacrifice but knows that he has made an even bigger one in giving up on the world. Rather than pondering his connections with others, he chains himself to work. He barely talks to his sister and mother and has a spotty relationship with a young woman who overstays her welcome. His only relationships of any interest are those with colleagues. His entire reality is built on money and the capitalist dreams of ascendancy it engenders. He refuses to be the failure his father turned out to be.

In the final story, "A Slender Back" ("Yaseta senaka"), a man named Ryōji faces his childhood home, now a prison of bereavement in anticipation of his father's funeral. As in "Galactic City," questions of mortality anticipate sobering answers. Although Ryōji blames his father for a troubled upbringing, he knows himself to be responsible for his future. From this emotional trauma he has emerged with what is easily the strongest bond in the entire book:

a friendship with the maternal figure this story's title describes. From the moment he sees her, there is a seemingly predestined connection between them. Ryōji sees firsthand what his father has done to her and carries that blame into the present. As a result, he loses interest in human connections and goes off on his own. He questions whether his father's behavior could be blamed on a cruel society or his own shortcomings.

Tatsushi and Ryōji are dealing with the deaths of their fathers, each in his own way. Tatsushi especially has been grappling with paternal failure since childhood. In essence, his life has been a desperate improvisation to avoid his father's thematic melody. He has seen what ambition can do to a person and knows that he must be careful in a system that would sooner suck him dry than offer material comfort. Just as we like to think that death brings out the truth in people, laying bare all the highs and lows of one's earthly transit in explicit detail, it also pushes the truth back. Tatsushi comes to realize this as he begins digging where he shouldn't. In learning the truth about his father, he learns the truth about himself. His roots may be gnarled, but at least they are his own.

Lingering in the background of all of this is World War II, a collective memory throughout the book's eponymous story, and which by extension implies a wealth of such personal narratives, fragmented and interspersed across a nation struggling in the aftermath. The war is an essential part of each family's history, Tatsushi's not least of all.[1] When he finally finds the relative he is looking for, it is in an all-but-forgotten complex of barracks housing left over from the war, reminding him of the upheavals

---

1. After the war, his grandfather returned from Manchuria with a prostitute, presaging a hostess industry that was booming by the 1980s, when this book was written.

whose ripples continue to reverberate in his subconscious. The choice of setting in "Galactic City" links back to postwar Japan, when snack bars were exclusively for US GIs of the Allied Occupation (1945–52) before being opened to the ones they occupied. Such establishments were melancholy stations of commerce for the "Mama-san" proprietresses who ran them. Sagisawa places one such character, referred to by Tatsuo by the more endearing "Oba-chan," at the center of the story. Oba-chan's bar has seen its fair share of faces comes and go, but a dedicated few remain in her care, such as it is. Less motherly than self-possessed, she has endured enough hardships to know that life is as fleeting and perishable as anything she serves to her customers. She speaks only when necessary and with the concise profundity of someone who understands that most words are wasted on the young. All that said, Sagisawa is by no means a cautionary writer hoping to instruct her readers with parables, but one teasing out people whose lives are forever altered by the ravages of global conflict, and who latch on to whatever sources of stability they can find, fleshly or otherwise.

Ryōji is a different case. His father's death doesn't so much sadden him as makes him aware of solitude. Said solitude has been his only consolation for four years, during which time he has constructed a tenuous facade of independence in the face of a boyhood that is forever trying to catch up. His life is uninteresting, his relationships even less so, and behind it all is his unfathomable affection for an emotionally unstable widow who hardly has room on her mental altar for his effigy. If anything, he seems to find more death in her living body than in his father's corpse. That she has a heartbeat does nothing to obscure the destruction she holds inside.

Given that *The Running Boy* was published in 1992 and written in the three years preceding, Sagisawa's characters wobble on the thinnest part of Japan's asset price bubble, which finally burst in 1990–91 when real estate and stock market inflation reached a point of oversaturation. Her stories shine valuable light on these developments. Tatsuo is a victim of his desire for financial success and seems to feel mocked by the gentrification taking place all around him. Ryōji's tale delves into the socioeconomic malaise of his generation and even describes his father as one whose "life had waxed and waned in concert with Japan's rapid growth and decline." As one of many unfortunate torchbearers of this historical downturn, he represents the simultaneous hope and alienation of modern subjectivity. Whether in Tatsuo's failed long-term investment in "Galactic City," the legal battle faced by Tatsushi in "The Running Boy," or the death of Ryōji's father in "A Slender Back," which prompts memories of a failed business and a man drowning in distractions, Sagisawa turns our attention toward the inevitability of degradation.

Such concerns fall under the wider metaphysical umbrella of a national identity crisis. At a practical level, snack bars like the Koyuki would surely have been gouged, as only die-hard locals would continue to frequent them while their younger counterparts were busy drowning in lack of foresight on the cusp of Japan's so-called Lost Decade. Yet warning signs of impending recession gifted Sagisawa with profound hindsight in return. Her evocation of an aging and declining population parallels a domino effect of bankruptcy, so prevalent that Tatsushi is able to build a thriving business on the failures of others. We see it reflected in the often-unfinished development projects in and around metropolitan centers and their trickle-down effect into rural areas.[2]

---

2. See Kenichi Ohno, *The History of Japanese Economic Development: Origins of Private Dynamism and Policy Competence* (London: Routledge, 2018), 162–78.

We may draw further parallels between the late 1980s and post-war Japan, when national self-confidence had eroded in tandem with economic stability. "More abstractly," writes Andrew Oros,

> [T]he death of the Showa emperor, Hirohito, in 1989 opened many troubling questions about past war responsibility that caused increased stress between Japan's more hawkish, nationalist right, which did not want the past to constrain Japan's progress toward a greater military role in the world, and the left, which feared that Japan's political system was not mature enough to prevent the kind of extremism that had led Japan to war five decades earlier. The end of the Cold War and the outbreak of the Persian Gulf War in 1991 opened political space for a renewed discussion about Japan's place in the world and whether the Cold War compromise of domestic antimilitarism was appropriate for the new Heisei era.[3]

Despite a lack of political commentary in *The Running Boy*, in light of this bit of history we may read Sagisawa's fixation on dead or dying father figures as more than coincidental.

This is just one of many themes shared by these stories. First, each is steeped in images of summer and heat, as if not only Japan but nature itself were an oppressive instrument in the sonata of everyday life. Second, dreams are integral to Sagisawa's protagonists, lending as much insight into their pasts as predicting their futures. Third, death marks not an end but a beginning. It opens Tatsuo's eyes to a convoluted destiny, turns Tatsushi's away from his own ego, and sets Ryōji on a path of hidden truth. The resulting flicker between "self" and "other" occurs so frequently that they become difficult to distinguish. Yet this sorrowful trio marches on, heading toward the same goal of knowing who they are. They are finite beings in a finite world. This fact alone compels them to live.

---

3. See Andrew L. Oros, *Normalizing Japan: Politics, Identity, and the Evolution of Security Practice* (Singapore: NUS, 2008), 71.

The blurring of "self" and "other" also compelled Sagisawa toward a tragic antithesis. On April 11, 2004, she took her own life at the age of thirty-five. Despite leaving behind more than twenty novels and short story collections, all of which brought her prodigious success and a dedicated readership, news of her death flew under media radars. The cause was initially reported as heart failure, but it was later revealed that she had hanged herself in her bathroom and was discovered by a friend late the next evening. Fans resisted this new information but resigned themselves to the truth when the thought of someone her age suffering heart failure was too unlikely to sustain. With that resignation came even harder-to-swallow speculations about the depression that drove her to suicide.

In her afterword for Sagisawa's autobiographical novel *My Story* (*Watashi no hanashi*, 2002), Junko Sakai characterizes Sagisawa as being confined by "quiet affection" (*shizukana aijō*). Although Sagisawa looked like a stylish urbanite, her favoring of wounded souls hinted at her own. Although it may not always be fruitful to profess knowledge of writers on a personal level through their fiction, we can be sure of knowing enough about Sagisawa's worldview as spoken through her characters. Episodes from her life bleed through almost every page. Like Sagisawa, the young couple at the center of *The Deceased* divorces after a year-long marriage. Lack of father figures, as discussed already, is another leitmotif, seen in "The Old Man of Jindaiji Temple" ("Jindaiji no ojii"), from her short story collection *Birds of the Sea, Fish of the Sky* (*Umi no tori, sora no sakana*, 1990), echoing the sudden death of her own father in February 1987—two months shy of her major literary debut. A genealogical discovery seems to have left the deepest footprint in her persona; when conducting personal interviews and research for a writing project, she learned that her paternal grandmother was Korean. This came as a shock to someone who had always identified herself as a Japanese writer, and thereafter nuanced her critique of social isolationism.

Armed with this knowledge, Sagisawa studied abroad in South Korea to learn the language when she was twenty-four. During and after her soul searching, she drew her Korean identity like a red thread through much of her creative output, even as she struggled to find a place to attach it.[4] The first such example occurs in "Fallen Blossoms" ("Hazakura no hi," 1990), from a short story collection of the same name, in which Masahiro, a young man who goes by "George," discovers he is of Zainichi status, meaning he was born of displaced Koreans mobilized during the Japanese occupation of Korea after World War II. *Polar Opposites* (*Saihate no futari*, 1996) is another example. This later novel details the unorthodox love affair between a middle-aged Zainichi Korean and a young Japanese American woman, further playing with notions of fragmented identities by filtering deterministic actions through the screen of romance.

However we choose to trace Sagisawa's double consciousness, we must also recognize that she came to it only by chance, unlike self-identified Zainichi writers. According to Yukiko Tsujiyama,

> The 1980s in which she grew up were a prosperous time for Japan, and success stories even among Zainichi Koreans were becoming less rare. South Korea had been democratized, and Japan-Korea relations were part of the everyday social landscape. It was a time when flagrant anti-Zainichi discrimination had receded into the shadows, to the point where people were ignorant of [Japan's colonial] history and the very existence of Zainichi citizens. One could

4. See, for example, Kōji Hayashi, *Sengo hinichi bungakuron* (Tokyo: Shinchōsha, 1997), 186–87, wherein Sagisawa is characterized as someone who was constantly "searching for a place to [which she might] return" (*kaereru basho o sagashiteiru*).

say that Megumu Sagisawa was a focal embodiment of Zainichi Koreans during this era.[5]

Tsujiyama's characterization is curious and leads us to question whether a perceived lack of overt discrimination might indicate a deeper internalization of racial oppression in the form of identity conflict. To be labeled as Zainichi is to be constantly in between national and ethnic categories. By the time Sagisawa wrote these stories, collective prejudices were embedded in the minds and bodies of third-generation Zainichi like herself. Their lack of overtness doesn't necessarily indicate an excess of stability.

Tsujiyama more rightly goes on to discuss Sagisawa's longing for a father figure, as expressed in *Do You Love Your Country?* (*Kimi wa kono kuni o suki ka*, 1997), also nominated for the Akutagawa Prize. In it, Ami is dealing with unresolved issues surrounding her upbringing as a sheltered Zainichi. She studies abroad in the United States, where she becomes fascinated by Hangul, the Korean syllabary, and goes on to attend a language school in Korea. She is the child of divorced parents and grew up without a father. Her attempts at connecting with a hyphenated self fail because she feels no connection to Korea as a country of her own. Still, she looks back on her immersion in the "mother tongue" as the happiest time of her life. At the end of the novel she achieves enough linguistic competency to satisfy her desire for connection, but Tsujiyama writes, "We understand that Ami seeks not a physical language but a mental one. Her search for a mother tongue exists only to make up for the lack of a father."[6]

5. Yukiko Tsujiyama, "Zainichi nisei/sansei no bungaku ni miru 'hahanarumono' to 'chichinarumono': Yan Sugiru, I Yanji, Sagisawa Megumu" (Symbols of Maternity and Paternity in the Work of Three Japan-Based Korean Writers: Yang Sok-il, Lee Yangii and Sagisawa Megumu), *Kyōritsu kokusai kenkyū* 32 (2015): 145.

6. Tsujiyama, "Zainichi nisei," 148.

According to Yoshihiro Harada, the exclusionary nature of Japanese society, compounded by an untenable Korean identity, delivered a one-two punch to Sagisawa's self-worth. He goes so far as to claim this as the seed of her depression. To readers, she was another Japanese writer but was far more complicated in her own image. Even after her death, netizens failed to acknowledge her "Koreanness," which may partly explain the lack of national attention to her death. "This awareness of both a Japanese and Korean self within her," Harada ventures, "led to violent internal conflict. She had no way of separating the two completely, and no one was the wiser." If only she had been able to determine once and for all that Korea was her true home, he concludes, she might still be alive.[7]

Although Sagisawa would have been the last to frame her death as martyrdom, questions of self-definition constitute an undeniable scaffolding of the depressions articulated in her work, and nowhere so poignantly as in this volume. It may not deal with Zainichi issues, but it does plumb depths of subject formation and genealogical convolution. Whatever one chooses to make of Sagisawa's Korean identity (or lack thereof), we may confidently read *The Running Boy* as a reflection of Japan's identity crisis in relation to economic collapse and collective war trauma. If anything, Sagisawa is proof that third-generation Zainichi were still affected by disruptions of World War II and the Occupation era.

In much the same way that watching a depressing film can lift the spirits by making us aware of how fortunate we are, *The Running Boy* provides underlying affirmation. It reminds us that even in the face of utter failure, we may never let go of our grandest

7. See https://plaza.rakuten.co.jp/haradayoshihiro/3002/ (accessed December 29, 2017).

aspirations. Realistic or not, we tend to them with urgency. There is little difference between our dreams and the real world—both are ephemeral. Accordingly, the challenges of this translation lie in bringing across Sagisawa's emotional mosaic with the sense of indelibility it deserves. Any intrusions on her whispers are therefore the result of my imperfect modulation. If anything came out of my experience in piecing it together, it was a realization that we are no more slaves to our environments than we are to ourselves. Like the boy in Tatsushi's dream, we are always running in life, but someday we must let the path give way until the waters of mortality consume us.

Galactic City

"Come on in," said Oba-chan, wiping down the countertop. Tatsuo looked away from the TV screen to the entrance.

A young couple had wandered into the bar. The tall, lean man sported an American baseball cap, the woman a bright orange polo shirt. They looked like students. Tatsuo snorted, unheard, and returned his attention to the TV.

Despite what the red lantern outside the door—*Koyuki Seasonal Cuisine*—would have one believe, the Koyuki was a dingy pub that served little more than cold tofu, grilled fish, and sake. Oba-chan was its sole proprietress. With only a single counter, it accommodated six, maybe seven people at most, though it was rarely full. Adjacent to the bar was a sitting room fitted with a low table and a TV. In the absence of customers, Oba-chan could be found reclining in front of it, popping peanuts and sipping away at her tea.

Despite having frequented the Koyuki for the past seven years, Tatsuo didn't think that Oba-chan had aged a bit. Sure, she might complain now and then about all the weight she had gained since quitting smoking, but those small, sunken eyes betrayed her indifference.

The couple sat together at the bar, looking over the sparse menu written up in the old lady's unexpectedly skillful hand. Oba-chan plunked down a pickled cucumber and seaweed salad. The young woman looked up.

"I'll have a beer, please." Then, to her companion: "Should we get some fish?"

"Anything, I'm famished."

"An order of saury it is, then, and some fried tofu . . ."

Tatsuo snorted again, listening to the couple's soft-spoken exchange. *Do us all a favor and take your business elsewhere*, he thought.

"Have you been here long?" said the woman in an effort to strike up a conversation as Oba-chan filled her glass.

"You might say that. Going on thirty years now."

The woman scanned the shop as if taking in a rare sight, ogling the faded, discolored posters on the walls and the oil-caked bottles of whisky lining the corner shelves.

"Wow . . . impressive . . ." she said under her breath.

Impressed, is she? Tatsuo mused to himself. *Good for her.*

"I'm guessing you don't see greenhorns like us very often?" said the man in the baseball cap.

Tatsuo nearly spit out his drink from laughter before finally managing to swallow it. *Look at him*, he thought. *A mere boy, barely over twenty, batting around words like "greenhorns."* It was all Tatsuo could do to suppress the bubbling in the pit of his stomach. It wasn't the first time, and he hated himself for giving into this feeling.

"Right you are. We've had nothing but regulars for as long as I've been open, but the past thirty years have taken their toll," the old lady answered with a grin before removing a plastic container of grated radish from the refrigerator.

"Oh, how's that?" the woman asked.

"They've all turned into doddering old fools. The rest are six feet under now. Once all my regulars are dead, this place will be empty."

By this last comment the young woman seemed taken aback, but the old lady continued chopping on the cutting board without missing a beat.

"Maybe it's time I started looking for new customers."

The young couple grew apathetically silent, nodding to each other for no apparent reason. The corners of Tatsuo's mouth curled into a bitter smile. By now, the ice in his drink had melted. He finished it off and got to his feet.

"Until next time."

"Sure thing," answered the old lady, not bothering to look up.

Tatsuo drew aside the shop curtain, stained enough to have been marinated in soy sauce, and stepped outside, enjoying the pleasant September winds wafting through his intoxication.

He made a turn at the public bathhouse on the corner and came out onto a narrow street. Gaps between the buildings afforded him a glimpse of the expressway's underside. Forming a roof over the main turnpike, it blocked out the sunlight by day and, at night, glowed so brightly it was almost eerie. He made his uncaring way forward.

Turnpike traffic was heavy, even at this time of night. In the corner of his eye, he watched the headlights rushing past him. The road was lined with skyscrapers. These buildings, none of which existed ten years ago, bristled the roadside as if guarding the asphalt they overshadowed, shielding what lay behind them from anyone traveling through. Those who merely sped along the turnpike on their way from points A to B knew nothing of the tangled streets beyond, let alone that customers of a small, empty pub were dropping like flies.

At one time, Tatsuo counted himself among those on the main line. That is, until he quit his job at a major trading company seven years back. He worked there for three years right out of college, his division operating out of one of these very buildings.

The modest apartment Tatsuo called home was located just ahead, nestled behind a newly opened supermarket. While it sometimes saddened him to realize he was over thirty and living in a place that didn't even have a running bath, he was too fed up with his own pessimism as of late to care. After failing to hold down a steady job, the promise of cheap rent was music to his ears.

As soon as he walked through the door, he kicked off his sandals and spread himself out on the floor mat. He was expecting a call from his girlfriend tonight.

Kyoko had been a secretary at the trading company. Since Tatsuo quit, she had moved on to other things, including her current stint at a Shinjuku nightclub. She was the only woman to ever show interest in Tatsuo, though nothing more than casual flirting had passed between them.

Eleven o'clock rolled around and the phone rang.

"Hello? It's me."

"Oh, hey."

"Were you sleeping?"

"No."

"Looks like I won't be able to make it tonight. I really wanted to stop by, you know."

"Did something come up?"

"No, it's not that . . ."

"I understand. Maybe next time? You know where to find me."

Kyoko had never been good at lying. She was neither particularly attractive nor intelligent, but perhaps that was what piqued his interest: she was living that same awkward life, and shared his faults to a T.

"Right," came her meek response before she hung up.

He sighed and repositioned himself face-up on the floor mat.

This wasn't the first time ineptness had saved her, but he was beginning to wish that she *would* just lie to him. At least he could be content in knowing he had been properly snubbed.

Having more time than he knew what to do with, he reached out a hand without getting up and turned on the television, which had been close to flatlining for months. Late-night reruns of crime dramas barely materialized through a grainy, distorted picture. He only heard the blare of police sirens and the voices of new talents spouting their lines so quickly that he couldn't even make out what they were saying.

He gave up, rolled over, and kicked off the set, plunging the palely lit room back into darkness. This left only the emergency exit sign from the rear of the supermarket to lend a morbid redness to his surroundings.

Too lazy to roll out the futon, he pulled over a neglected pillow from the corner with his foot and drifted off to sleep in his jeans. For no apparent reason, in his drunken haze he thought of the Koyuki interior. The pub was growing lonelier with the death of each loyal customer, and tonight more than ever he felt the strange tragedy of it all.

Tatsuo learned of Yamazaki's death a few days later.

With nothing else to do, he made a rare early appearance at the Koyuki, only to be met with the usual suspects: Ōshita, Nogawa, and Gan, as well as the old retiree who ran a wallpaper shop and was known affectionately among the group as the "Dean."

"Oh, you're all here," he said as he came in.

Everyone turned around with a start. It was then he noticed Ōshita and Nogawa were dressed for a funeral. He froze with his hand on the shop curtain.

"What is it?"

The others only hung their heads in silence to his question. Their beer bottles were wet with condensation and the countless water rings they left on the bar glittered strangely beneath the fluorescent ceiling fixture. Even the light itself seemed a shade darker in the hot, humid air.

"What is it?" Tatsuo repeated.

Again, no response.

"Anyone want to tell me what's going on?"

"He's dead, that fool," Nogawa answered through clenched teeth. "A stroke."

"Yamazaki, you mean?"

Ōshita nodded in silence.

"But . . . he seemed fine the last time I saw him."

Nogawa turned to the side and spat out his words.

"That's what makes it so damn hard to swallow."

Tatsuo stood in a daze. At a loss for words, he looked to Oba-chan for clarity. She wiped down the counter in front of an empty stool and put out a fresh glass.

"Don't just stand there, take a seat," she said, and poured him a beer.

Tatsuo did as he was told, looking around at the others in disbelief. Ōshita and Nogawa, the latter wearing a black suit in lieu of his go-to drabbery, held up weary faces. Gan, who ran a drainpipe construction supplier not a quarter of a mile down from the Koyuki, crossed his bronzed arms and closed his eyes, while the hollow-cheeked old Dean stared at the Koyuki ceiling in a stupor.

A snapshot of Yamazaki, taken out for the occasion, stood propped by a plastic chopstick holder on the bar top.

The Dean turned to Tatsuo.

"Join us in a farewell toast, won't you?" he said hoarsely.

Tatsuo turned to the photo and lifted his glass to pay respects.

"It should've been *my* turn to go," the Dean said offhandedly.

Tatsuo quickly downed his beer and was about to refute this foolish statement, but he, like Oba-chan and the rest, remained silent. He hung his head, unable to say more. The Dean had just turned seventy this year.

"It can't go on like this," Gan said with little conviction.

Gan's "turn," as the Dean had put it, wasn't too far off, either.

Tatsuo fiddled with his empty glass, unnerved by the whole conversation. Carbonation from the beer gurgled in his stomach.

"Us dying off like this . . . it's like we're just lights going out, one by one," added Ōshita.

The Dean was seventy and Gan in his early sixties, but Ōshita, Nogawa, and the late Yamazaki all looked to be about the same age.

Tatsuo remembered hearing that the younger three were old college buddies who had been frequenting the Koyuki since their student days.

From what he knew, each had his part to play. Yamazaki and Nogawa were the perfect comedic partners, and Ōshita the silent onlooker. Nogawa, ever the serious one, no longer had goofy Yamazaki to play off of. At first glance, this hapless trio would have seemed nothing more than a few know-nothing businessmen past their prime, but in the Koyuki they were in their element as they swapped tales of better days. When he was still alive, Yamazaki enjoyed few things more than reminiscing about the past.

—*Call her "Mama," Tatsuo.*

Yamazaki had taken issue with the way Tatsuo called the owner "Oba-chan," a rather intimate title reserved for older women, and would chide him about it at every opportunity.

Since the Dean and Gan were locals, a comfort zone three decades in the making awaited them in the Koyuki. It was only seven years ago that Tatsuo had first walked through its door, making him a relative newcomer among the regulars. The others had earned their right to address the old lady on familiar terms.

Though Yamazaki had been a mild-mannered man, especially compared to Nogawa with his ceaseless scowl, and had a soft spot for Tatsuo, he was always chiding the younger man for calling her "Oba-chan," and would frown whenever he corrected him.

"Yamazaki used to have the hots for Mama, that schmuck," said Nogawa.

"Hmm, you may be right," the old lady answered in her typically blunt manner.

"Now that I think of it . . . when was it now? Oh yes, during our big game back at university."

"Yes, yes, that was one for the books," added Ōshita.

Another of their stories, it seemed, was winding up for the pitch.

"Remember? Mama brought us lunch boxes when I told her about the game."

Tatsuo had never heard this one before. He inadvertently looked at Ōshita, unable to imagine Oba-chan doing anything of the sort. By the fervency with which the Dean and Gan nodded, grinning all the while, it was clear they remembered it well.

"I don't know about your generation, but in my day those students were all a bunch of hooligans. Country bumpkins, all of 'em. The girls were clueless, too. Fresh off the farm."

"Is that right?"

"So, you can imagine the commotion when a looker like our 'Mama' here came to cheer on Yamazaki."

Tatsuo had grown accustomed to their embellishments, but was a bit surprised to hear the old lady being referred to as a "looker," let alone her cheering like some crazed fan at a ballgame.

"Yamazaki was a pitcher back then. He was ninth up to bat. They were down two outs. No one expected a miracle, and the batting line-up for the next inning looked promising."

Nogawa was getting tipsy, his face red as a baboon. He propped himself up on the bar.

"But I tell ya, Yamazaki must've taken Mama's cheering to heart, because so help me if he didn't knock one right out of the park."

"He hit a home run?"

Ōshita and Nogawa smiled and nodded in unison.

"His batting average wasn't even .100, but man did he come through."

"That home run came out of nowhere. It won us the game."

"You should've seen the way the girls eyed Mama at lunch after the game, jealousy written all over their faces."

"Yep, he was always popular with the ladies."

"Really? *Our* Yamazaki?"

"You bet, he was quite the star."

It was one thing to imagine the old lady as her attractive younger self, but Yamazaki? A star? Tatsuo sighed, trying his best to take it all in. Nogawa glared back at him with drunken eyes.

"Oh, you should've seen him back then. He was really quite fit."

"Really, Tatsuo," Gan chimed in. "He was a good-looking man. He could've been an actor. Now he just looks like a fat prune."

This made everyone laugh, though only for a moment, since the only way Yamazaki existed in the present tense was in the photograph.

The Dean's laughter faded into a fit of coughing. The corners of his eyes were glistening. It must have been contagious, as it wasn't long before everyone was in tears. Nogawa plunked his flushed face onto the counter and wept.

Ōshita patted him on the back with one hand and wiped away his own tears with the back of the other. He took away the honorary beer from in front of the makeshift memorial and drank it down.

"Mama, another round for Yamazaki," he said, raising the empty glass.

The old lady plucked it expressionlessly from his hand and jerked open the refrigerator door. She uncapped a new beer with a *psssht* that sounded oddly out of place.

Tatsuo wiped his sweat in the Koyuki's stagnant air.

That night, watching Ōshita and Nogawa staggering home down the alleyways, it was as if nothing had changed, save for the mourning attire and absence of the man for whom it was being worn. Even as Tatsuo watched them through vacant eyes, he couldn't help thinking they had been left behind.

Tatsuo stepped inside his apartment to a ringing phone. It was Kyoko. She hadn't called in a while, but as someone who was more or less being supported by her, he wasn't about to argue.

"How's things?" she blurted out, clearly drunk.

"Fine. What's up?"

"Nothing much. Do I need a reason to call you?"

"Not at all."

"Any luck finding work?"

"No."

It wasn't that he hadn't found a job; he just hadn't gone looking for one.

She burst into tears, breaking his long silence.

"Hey, what's wrong?"

"It's nothing."

She hung up without so much as a "bye" or "see you." It wasn't the first time, and it hurt to hear her like this. He clicked his tongue and returned the receiver to its cradle.

He spread himself out in the middle of the room, deep in thought. It had been six or seven years since Kyoko started hostessing in Shinjuku. Aside from the fact that she wasn't all that appealing, it was beyond him why she continued working in a place where she obviously didn't fit. He didn't want to think it was because of him. He also knew there wasn't a single thing he could do about it either way.

She had gone to work for the trading company straight out of junior college, leaving it when he quit seven years ago, as if in solidarity. Tatsuo counted on his fingers. *Yes . . . she must be pushing her thirties, too.*

He took a deep breath, feeling a weight easing up off his chest.

His eyes burned in the sallow fluorescent light. One of the tubes was shorting out, blinking sporadically with a hollow click. He had neglected it for a long time, even knowing how bad it was on the eyes. The light was on its way out, ready to die. *Indeed, why prolong the suffering when you can just get it over with*, he thought, wrapping his body in a summer quilt.

The thin coverlet provided little relief, but he was too lazy to get another. The light continued its battle. Tatsuo gave his legs a good stretch and finally dragged himself to the light switch to shut it off.

Despite graduating from a reputable school and settling into a coveted corporate job, his inevitable termination had a reason all its own. Put simply, he had been cheated. There wasn't a doubt in his mind, though any resentment he once felt had by now shriveled up.

In any case, his life took a fateful turn when he received a telephone call seven years back from a college classmate. He and some friends were starting up a new business venture and wanted Tatsuo in. Tatsuo expressed an interest in meeting with him to work out the details.

Sometime later, he came to Tatsuo's office personally. He dropped a handful of pamphlets on his desk and told Tatsuo to "look them over." The pamphlets were filled with pictures of vast green meadows. On the facing page, printed in large yellow letters:

TREES OF HAPPINESS!
WHY HAVEN'T *YOU* STAKED YOUR CLAIM IN
THE BEAUTIFUL HOKKAIDO WILDERNESS?

He explained the venture as follows. Investors were expected to buy two acres of prime land near the untended forests of Hokkaido, where saplings would be planted. With only a nominal monthly service charge, in twenty years the saplings would grow into magnificent trees worth upwards of five million yen. The man fervently assured Tatsuo of a surefire investment and that he had nothing to lose.

Having been at the company for three years, Tatsuo had finally been entrusted with more important business matters. He was busy enough with his own work and only agreed to help out because of his classmate's repeated assurance that he was doing him a favor for old time's sake.

He distributed the pamphlets to his coworkers and even gave one to his boss, who held Tatsuo in particularly high esteem and agreed to buy ten shares. When Tatsuo reported his success, his friend was in tears.

—*You're a lifesaver, I owe you one. I can't thank you enough.*

It would be a lie to say that Tatsuo didn't feel a private sense of superiority at that moment. But it was no match for the price he would later have to pay.

Sure enough, the land titles were remitted once his coworkers' money was deposited into a reserve account. Tatsuo had been suspicious of the unusually low prices, but attributed them to the remoteness of the land in question. Naturally, he was all the more relieved when his deed showed up in the mail.

It was then that Kyoko rang him.

—*Something about this isn't right,* she began. *I'm from Hokkaido, so believe me when I tell you: the addresses on the deed and the pamphlet just don't match up. That place is right near a volcano. Not a single blade of grass grows there.*

He felt like he had hit by a truck. The blood drained from his head.

He tried calling the contact number printed on the business card, only to be informed by a robotic loop that the number was no longer in service. He contacted other college acquaintances, but none knew of the man's whereabouts. Even worse, they had all fallen prey to the same scheme.

More than half of his coworkers were entangled in this act of fraud. The total damages, including his own investment, amounted to millions.

Having no other choice, he left the company of his own accord.

Since then he had drifted between jobs, never staying at any one for long. At first, he did this intentionally in hopes of tracking down the one who put him in this situation. And even if the opportunity for revenge never presented itself, he would be happy at least saying his piece. Not the most civilized way to go about it, perhaps, but it reflected a blazing, tenacious desire that lived and breathed like a small kernel inside him.

And then, before he knew it, his hatred stopped. Resignation had gradually eaten away at his heart until it got the best of him.

His flame of hatred was flickering out. It was the only way to make peace.

"Hey, Dean, is that you?"

It was a drizzly day, the morning news awash with reports of this year's unusually rainy autumn.

Tatsuo was on his way to buy cigarettes. His sandals were soaked with sewer water collecting in the pot-holed asphalt. He glanced down at his own soiled feet and gave up, deliberately splashing through the puddles.

As he made his way over to the wallpaper shop, he called out again to the Dean, who was standing under a black umbrella.

"What are you doing?"

The Dean's shop was on a corner off the main drag. Its dusty interior was stacked with enormous reams of wallpaper, not a customer in sight. To the left of the shop was a large pachinko parlor with a perpetually lit neon sign, and the white tile-mounted highrise on the right formed an alley between them. Being sandwiched by such monstrosities made the modest shop appear abandoned and forgotten.

He stared at his shop, turning slowly in response.

"Oh . . . Tatsuo. Take a look."

"Why?"

"This shop was opened sixty years ago, but in all that time I never noticed just how miserable it is."

"I see . . ."

"It's quite dark out for this time of day," said the Dean. The street was congested with the din and exhaust fumes of passing trucks. The expressway loomed over it like a veil, catching the sunlight and casting the low-rise buildings along the turnpike in virtual darkness. He blinked his weary eyes, looking up at the rainwater dripping from the expressway, but soon returned his gaze to the shop.

"Well, it *is* raining today, so it's more overcast than usual," Tatsuo mumbled, unable to think of anything better to say.

The Dean faced him with a grin, exposing the abyss of a toothless mouth. Rain dripped audibly from the eaves and onto the cardboard boxes stacked outside the store. The boxes were stuffed with reams of wallpaper. *Half Rolls 500 Yen Each* was scrawled on the sides. He looked down and let out a faint sigh before carrying the boxes inside in his scrawny arms.

"I'm losing," he said with his back to Tatsuo.

"To what?"

The Dean shut the door with a clatter. It was unclear whether he hadn't heard the question or was just ignoring it.

Tatsuo didn't budge. He squinted at the concrete monstrosity snaking through the sky beyond his vinyl umbrella.

The rain-slicked expressway revealed only the eerie skeletal structure of its underbelly to those below.

The highway blocked out the sun during the day, but when night fell the streetlights illuminated the surrounding area. He suddenly remembered the words Kyoko had told him one night, looking out at the expressway.

—*It's like a light trap, isn't it?*

—*How's that?*

—*Because these filthy towns close in on it from either side, like they're attracted to the highway somehow.*

—*It's the other way around.*

—*Huh?*

—*The towns were already here before the highway was built.*

—*But isn't it all the same?*

—*I don't follow.*

—*Moths are the first to fly.*

—*Yes, I see what you mean. So that makes me a filthy moth drawn to the light?*

Kyoko didn't answer. Her profile was strangely pale, like hard china, and had remained firmly implanted in his memory ever since.

The rain pared down to a drizzle, but continued until nightfall. Kyoko obviously wasn't coming, and he was hungry besides. He slipped on his sandals, thinking he might make his way over to the Koyuki. The moment his hand touched the doorknob, the phone rang.

"It's me, Kyoko."

Wasted again.

"Oh, hey."

"I'm coming over."

"Okay."

"On second thought, maybe not."

He frowned.

"What are you talking about?'

"Say, what would you do if I told you I couldn't come?"

"What would I do . . .?"

He never knew how to act when she got like this.

"Well, what would you do?" She was really out of it this time. "I'm talking to you. Say something." Her tone suddenly grew harsh. "Say something. Tell me to come, tell me not to come, tell me anything."

"Kyoko . . .?"

"I'm desperate here. I have no idea what you think about your life. I want someone to depend on, too."

He didn't know what to say.

"I'm too tired now, anyway. I used to think it was okay to feel tired, but now I get exhausted just thinking about it."

"Kyoko."

She went silent. The only sounds coming through the receiver were car horns in the background, but even these disappeared with the plinking of dropping coins, leaving him with a cold dial tone in his ear.

He sat for a long time in the darkness of his room with the receiver in one hand. Something inside him stopped breathing again. *I want someone to depend on, too . . .*

Kyoko's voice rang in his head. He wondered if he wasn't depending on something. Perhaps the bone-dry emotion within him, if nothing else.

The exit sign behind the supermarket spilled into his room with its persistent red glow. An ambulance siren filled the streets outside his window.

—*Call her "Mama," Tatsuo.*

Tatsuo turns to see Yamazaki in his white baseball uniform. Yamazaki rubs his belly regretfully

—*Am I loose in the cage or what?*

He is standing in a dusty athletic field. A clear day. Nogawa is jumping up and down in the background.

Tatsuo tries calling out to him, but no voice comes. Impatiently, he walks over to him.

—*What's wrong? What are you doing?* he says when he finally reaches him.

—*See, I told you, she's a beauty!*

Nogawa wears that same baboonish grin he always does when drunk.

He turns to see Oba-chan in the stands, only to find she is the same old lady he has always known, those beady little eyes nestled in the folds of her chubby face.

He hurries to the stands, and hears a woman's voice behind him.

—*Third up, number eight. Ōshita, shortstop.*

He glances back at the field.

—*Ah.*

Ōshita is at the plate, brandishing his bat—not in a white uniform, but his familiar drab suit.

Tatsuo notices that Yamazaki and Nogawa are in their usual brown.

Even with a pitcher nowhere in sight, a fastball comes hurtling toward the plate. Ōshita swings hard and misses. The force of it knocks him on his rear.

No one laughs. Ōshita only scratches his head and smiles to himself.

—*There was a time when we were all alive,* the old lady mutters nearby.

—*Huh? What do you mean by that?*

Ignoring Tatsuo's question, she repeats herself.

—*There was a time when we were all alive . . .*

Tatsuo awoke in red light. He sat upright and gazed blankly at the floor mat.

Though still half asleep, he didn't feel like staying inside. When he looked at the clock, it was ten on the dot. He hadn't slept long.

Outside, the rain had stopped. Tatsuo left his umbrella by the door and made his listless way down the alleyway. The evening breeze caressed him warmly.

Kyoko's phone call mingled with the dream inside his head. He was certain she would never call him again.

"'Trees of Happiness,' my ass," he grumbled as he made his un-steady way down the rain-slicked asphalt.

Gan was sitting at the bar inside the Koyuki and hadn't expected to see Tatsuo there. Tatsuo took the adjacent seat at Gan's request. The moment he sat down, he was overcome with fierce hunger.

The same woman who had left him with those odd words in his dream now offered him a small dish of kidney beans boiled in soy sauce. Tatsuo wolfed them down at once. Gan cast him a wry glance.

"Hey Tatsuo, did you hear?"

"Hear what?"

"About the wallpaper shop."

Tatsuo remembered the Dean standing alone in the rain earlier that morning.

"You mean the Dean's . . .?"

"It's terrible."

"How so? He didn't look that bad to me."

Gan peered deeply into Tatsuo's face.

"You saw him?"

"Yeah, this morning."

"And how was he?"

"Well, I only chatted with him briefly outside the shop," Tatsuo answered with difficulty.

"In that downpour?"

"Yeah."

"What was he doing?"

"Actually, he was just staring at his store."

Gan sighed melodramatically.

"I imagine things must be hard for him."

"What? Why?"

Oba-chan placed a drink in front of Tatsuo and gazed up at a corner of the ceiling.

"The wallpaper shop is going to be torn down to make way for new construction."

"The son insisted and he finally gave in."

"Oh, that would explain it."

Tatsuo thought of the Dean's figure at the shop, his back turned, his talk of giving up.

"I guess there's nothing we can do."

"Mm," mumbled Oba-chan, still focused on the ceiling.

Tatsuo suddenly imagined her at the peak of her beauty, and the Dean in his prime.

Even as the two of them sat in the stale air, he imagined a time when the Koyuki was brimming with the vigor and camaraderie of young men. This little bar had seen its fair share of seasons come and go, and he sensed traces of those years and months lodged in every cranny. The feeling of it brought into focus the words Oba-chan had spoken in his dream.

He put his head in his hands and sighed.

"You've all been dead for a long time," he muttered under his breath.

Neither Oba-chan nor Gan seemed to catch it.

The old lady looked to the entrance.

"Welcome," she said in her disagreeable voice.

A young woman sat herself on the chair opposite the two men.

Gan stood up as if this was his cue and left the bar, grumbling about how tired he was. He sympathized much with the Dean, who had agreed to shut down his shop under pressure from his son. Gan, too, would be leaving the drainpipe business to his own son. Perhaps the whole situation had hit a little too close to home for him.

Now that he was essentially alone at the Koyuki, Tatsuo gazed in the young woman's direction, but not at her directly.

"I'm famished, but didn't feel much like cooking," she said with a smile by way of breaking the ice. She ordered a beer, some chicken poppers, and pan-fried noodles.

It was then that Tatsuo realized something. It was her. He remembered the woman in the orange polo shirt who had accompanied that tall gruff man in the baseball cap. Here she was again, only now she had on a loose men's cotton shirt that shaved a few years off her face.

"You know, Oba-san, I was wondering this the last time I was here, too, but what's this 'Electric Brandy' you keep advertising?" she said, picking at her kidney beans. Tatsuo grinned inwardly. Had Yamazaki been alive to see this, no doubt he would have urged her to call the old lady "Mama."

"It's brandy and curaçao. Pretty strong stuff."

"Huh, sure is a weird name," the woman said, almost to herself. Tatsuo faced her abruptly.

"Won't you try some?"

The moment the words came out, he wondered why he said them at all. Maybe it was because he felt somehow close to her by the way she addressed the old lady as "Oba-san."

She looked unsure, but after a moment smiled and nodded.

The old lady took out her bottle of Electric Brandy and poured the oddly colored liquid into a small, toy-like glass.

"Wow, it's really sweet," she said, savoring this new flavor. "Mind if I join you?" Not waiting for Tatsuo's answer, she moved over to the stool next to him. "I'm in no mood to eat here all by myself," she added with a carefree smile.

She wolfed down the food before her with a healthy appetite.

"Age?"

"You mean how old am I?"

"Yes."

"Nineteen."

Whatever "closeness" Tatsuo had felt toward her crumbled away.

"Nineteen," he echoed, blowing out a puff of cigarette smoke.

"Pretty young, huh?" she said, anticipating his next words. She looked at him as if to say, *I know what you're thinking.*

Holding chopsticks in her right hand and twirling a long lock of hair with her left, she glared wryly at Tatsuo. He gave a bitter smile in return without meaning to.

"What happened to your boyfriend?"

The young woman's face went blank again. She looked at Tatsuo for a long time before flashing him a smile.

"Oh stop it, he's not my boyfriend."

"But don't you live together?"

"Where'd you get that idea?"

"I just assumed."

"I admit, your powers of observation are pretty sharp. But it's not like that. That kid was just crashing at my apartment at the time."

The fact that she could have that kind of relationship with someone and not be romantically involved was typical of her age, yet her referring to him as a "kid" made Tatsuo feel strangely renewed.

Once she was done eating, the woman pushed her beer bottle, still a third filled, over to him.

"Finish this. I'm stuffed."

"How about another Electric Brandy?"

"Sure," she answered, almost fawning, and drew nearer to him.

She had an intoxicating scent. Her shampoo, maybe. Every time the woman's head came closer, her fragrance lingered in his nostrils. Oba-chan was uncapping a bottle away from them.

Midnight rolled around and the old lady began to clear away their glasses.

"Show's over, you two."

Tatsuo and the young woman got up from their small stools and went outside, their heads bobbing like buoys on waves of drunkenness.

The storm clouds had dispersed, revealing a multitude of stars in the autumnal sky high above the clean breeze. The sky had a clarity all its own after the rain. There was a slight chill in the air.

The woman slipped her arm through his as they turned at the bathhouse and came out onto the byroad that led to the main drag, giving Tatsuo another whiff of her scent. In his lush haze, he saw the expressway glowing dimly through the narrow gaps between the buildings that barred his way.

"They're like stars," the woman said absentmindedly.

He looked at her face, wondering what she was going on about. He followed her gaze to the expressway lights.

"My eyes are bad," she went on, "but one advantage of poor eyesight, I think, is that everything looks much more beautiful at night."

"Stars, you say?"

"Yeah. They're all blurred together, kind of like the Milky Way."

"The Milky Way?"

"You don't think so?"

He took a moment to swallow the uneasy feeling in silence.

"Do you see it?" she persisted, holding his face in her gaze.

He squinted at the lights.

"I once knew a woman who referred to those same lights as a light trap."

"A light trap? Why?"

He vaguely recalled what Kyoko had said about the small, filthy things swarming around those lights. Realizing the meaning might be lost out of context, he felt an indefinable anxiety rise up violently from the pit of his stomach to the back of his throat.

"I've often wondered that myself," he said, swallowing the thought back inside. And suddenly, that little insect he had felt wriggling around inside him since the woman put her arm in his went still and disappeared altogether.

The scent of this young woman's hair was something Kyoko didn't have. Oba-chan's offhanded comment on that chalked field crossed his mind: *There was a time when we were all alive.* Yamazaki was truly gone. The wallpaper shop had gone under. And not least of all, the Koyuki itself had long withered away.

"But I can see the stars . . . like a river of light across the autumn sky," the woman said, turning the words into a melody.

"A river of light?"

She was still looking out at the expressway with an air of enchantment.

"Yes."

"How do you mean?"

"Like I said, the Milky Way. In the old days people used to call it a river of light, you know."

At that moment, she slipped herself free of his arms just as effortlessly as she had entangled herself in them and staggered ahead. She waved an index finger, humming to herself. *Quite a character*, Tatsuo thought.

He realized he was mistaken in thinking she was a college student. Living out her life as she was in a town where light was overtaken by development, the woman who likened these rows of lights to the Milky Way was somehow pitiful in Tatsuo's eyes.

As they walked together, the expressway lights—far brighter than the countless stars overhead—threw their long shadows across the asphalt, drifting like dead leaves borne along by the wind.

Tatsuo stepped outside. It was getting cold, and he had forgotten his windbreaker back at the Koyuki after an especially chilly late summer evening some weeks earlier.

It was approaching midnight, but he was far from tired. With nothing better to do, he left his apartment and headed for the pub, going his usual way. When he passed the bathhouse, he saw that the Koyuki's red lantern wasn't lit. Thinking Oba-chan had closed early, he placed a hand on the shop curtain.

A weak light wavered beyond the stained cloth.

He was about to slip through, but stopped himself upon hearing a low murmur coming from inside.

"Katchin, Jūkichi, Nori-chan, Yama-chan, Hideyoshi, Kida-san, Kait-chan, Mat-chan, Takabō, Kuni-san, Hirarin, Mura-san, Akabē . . ."

It was the old lady's voice. He entered and peered into the TV room.

She was reclining on the floor mat as she always did when there weren't any customers, staring at something spread out on the low table. She merely sat there, not turning to greet him, though he was sure she was aware of his presence.

"Oba-chan . . . what are you doing?"

"If you're here for your jacket," she said, still not bothering to turn around, "I put it over there."

He looked over to the bar and saw his windbreaker rolled up on a stool. He picked it up, then knelt down at the sitting room entrance and let his eyes wander to the table.

The old lady was looking at an old musty album. A smell like that of secondhand books filled his nose.

"What are you doing here all alone?" he said. He tried to get a closer look at the antique brown album and the many black-and-white pictures glued and mounted inside. "What are those, Oba-chan?"

He knew the answer even as he said it. One of the photographs showed two rows of young men clad in white baseball uniforms.

"Just some old photos."

Yamazaki was front row center. He was unmistakable. Far from the pot-bellied man he had dreamed of, this Yamazaki was clean-cut with a gleaming smile. There was an innocence about him.

Ōshita and Nogawa were also among them. Next to the uniformed men were a smiling Dean in his forties and Gan with rolled-up jacket sleeves, exposing muscular arms.

"How did you get these? Aren't they . . .?" he said, gazing at the pictures.

But the old lady didn't answer.

"I've come to a decision. I'm closing the bar at the end of the month," she said bluntly.

He looked at her in silence. She didn't bother facing him, though her eyes seemed to flit in his direction for a moment, and quickly got to her feet. She went behind the counter and started on the dishes.

Tatsuo stood on his knees and looked around the pub.

"You're serious about this?"

The old lady nodded.

"I can't very well stand all night, or I'll stop moving altogether."

He was still for a while in the sticky air, with only the sound of running water to cut through the Koyuki's silence, in which time seemed frozen.

He got to his feet and went to the other side of the counter.

"There's something I've always wanted to ask you," he said.

She continued washing dishes in silence.

"Why did you name this place 'Koyuki'?"

The old lady wrung out her washcloth and washed the sink for a long while.

"Actually . . . it's my name," she answered at last.

He laughed slightly. Many thoughts passed through his mind, from the breathtaking figure cheering in the bleachers to the presumed many who had passed through the Koyuki's doors vying for her attentions.

"I see," he murmured.

As he left the Koyuki, nearly all of the lights in the small back alley shops had been extinguished. As he turned at the bathhouse onto the narrow road, once again the expressway came into view, aglow with its multitude of lights.

—*You've all been dead for a long time.*

He didn't know whether he said this aloud or in his heart.

The lights pulled him along and a low voice repeated itself endlessly inside him in rhythm with his pace.

—*Katchin, Jūkichi, Nori-chan, Yama-chan, Hideyoshi, Kida-san, Kait-chan, Mat-chan, Takabō, Kuni-san, Hirarin, Mura-san, Akabē*

. . .

The expressway towered over him, looking down on his staggering figure.

He had an urge to run, but continued making his unsteady way down the road.

The Running Boy

A high concrete wall stands in the boy's way.

He doesn't know where he's come from or where he's running to. All he does know is that this scream is tearing him apart. The boy has pedaled all the way here, spurred on by something, or someone, unseen.

He straddles a rusted monstrosity of a bicycle. Shorter than his peers, he struggles to keep his balance and comes to a clattering halt.

Racing alongside the concrete wall, he notices a breeze spilling over from the other side, intermingled with the scent of the tide. After a long stretch with no visible end, the wall bends into a hook. There *must* be ocean beyond it.

He hops off his bicycle and faces the intricately cracked wall.

The sun shines brightly at his feet. His surroundings are quiet, but a faint breeze flutters in his ears.

He turns to see an elevated train station bathed in sun. He faces the wall with renewed determination and heads for the station. He looks up and squints into the morning glare.

As he approaches, brightness gives way to gloomy and chilly air until even the station is steeped in gray. He eyes the platform.

A cool wind skims across its bare surface, and he imagines himself standing up there in the shade. He notices a figure standing on the platform: a man holding a child's hand. The child has a backpack slung across his shoulders and a small straw hat on his head. He grips the man's hand tightly.

The boy tries to make out the man's face. Sweat pours from his armpits, his cheeks, his forehead. It trickles down like oil. He has never felt lonelier.

He calls out as loud as he can.

—*Sensei! Katō-sensei!*

The man notices him, filling the boy's heart with a ray of light.

Katō-sensei purses his lips. He seems to recognize the boy. This chance encounter, this single moment of connection, alone in these unfamiliar streets by the sea, is enough to give the boy temporary respite from solitude.

Katō-sensei raises a hand and smiles, exposing the fanged incisors that earned him the nickname "Mr. Dracula."

He calls down, his voice light and carefree.

—*It's been a long time. Everything going well, I take it?*

—*How can I get up there? By train?*

Holding on to this glimmer of hope, he implores his former homeroom teacher with such desperation that blood threatens to gush from his throat at any moment. But the man's face darkens.

—*Hmm, what to do. I don't think the train runs that way . . .*

—*What if I rode up on my bike? How long would it take?*

Katō-sensei takes a moment to calculate.

—*Forty or fifty minutes, I'd say.*

—*Oh.*

The boy wants to cry.

—*I don't think I can make it.*

But make it for what? He doesn't know.

The boy bids a quick farewell and returns to his bicycle by the wall, which only now he realizes is nothing more than a levee. He was simply too close to see it. Sure enough, just beyond it, he spots a group of masts jutting eerily into the sky.

A piercing siren fills the air, laden with the distinctive scent of sunshine.

He scans the area and notices a small shop he overlooked in his haste. He makes his way to what little shade it has to offer him.

The light shining through the awning imbues it with the same sienna as all the other storefronts. It appears to be a cheap candy shop, or perhaps a general store. Inside, a young storekeeper disinterestedly kneads a lump of dough.

—*Excuse me . . .*

The boy has his heart in his mouth. The storekeeper stops what he is doing and looks up.

—*Which way should I go? I'm, uh . . .*

The young storekeeper doesn't even wait for the boy to finish before going back to his kneading, answering curtly:

—*Just keep going along the canal.*

—*Oh?*

When the boy repeats the question, the storekeeper stops what he is doing and steps outside, clapping flour off his hands. He seems unfazed by the interruption.

—*The canal, huh?*

Following the storekeeper's gaze, the boy turns to the same stretch of concrete and the countless masts sticking out from behind it.

—*There's a path under the levee. Just follow it and you'll get there.*

He squints into the glare.

—*But . . .*

The road ends where the wall angles off.

The boy turns to find the storekeeper already gone. He peers inside the shop, seeing only a misshapen lump of dough.

He returns to his rusted bicycle. It's lying on the ground, back wheel still spinning with a rhythmic squeak.

He reaches the spot where the levee is shortest, the only place he has any chance of climbing. He grips the wall with all his might. Pieces of concrete crumble away, grazing his forehead on their way down. He finds a foothold and inches his way up, enduring the dust in his eyes. His fingertips turn pale and grow numb with each desperate grip in whatever indentations he is able to find.

After what seems like forever, he clambers his way to the top. The levee is a meter wide, giving him room to lay himself out to regain strength.

The boy puts his cheek to the hot concrete, while beyond him innumerable waves sparkle in the sunlight. The water's surface has a certain thickness to it. He remembers the canal the shopkeeper mentioned. He sits up and looks out through a filter of eyelashes.

The stagnant canal water is slick with green, pockets of sunlight glittering here and there like upturned fish bellies. The levee overlooks the canal bank. A mountain of wooden barrels lies stacked at the base. A row of lichen-covered planks floats parallel to the levee, forming a long and buoyant walkway across the water.

The boy stands atop the levee and shields his eyes, looking out at the endless row of planks.

The early summer sun glitters harshly off the water, casting webs of shimmering white light upon him. Seized by a desire to go wherever it might lead, he feels it like a needle burrowing through him.

He swallows back his trepidation and jumps down lightly onto one of the planks. To avoid sinking, he immediately jumps to the next one, and the next. He sprints with all his might along the narrow walkway.

Some of his steps send sprays of water on his knees. He tries supporting himself by holding on to the barrels at his left, only to find that they, too, are floating. To his right there is nothing, save for the light undulating on the water's surface.

With even less certainty, he runs as fast as his feet will carry him. He runs and runs, ignoring his soaked clothing and the threat, so near, of sinking into the depths.

—*I need to keep going . . .*

These words course through him like a never-ending melody. Is it his voice that speaks them, or someone else's? He runs with the wind, trying not to let the planks give way beneath him.

Official documents were designed to be emotionless. And yet, here was Tatsushi, walking through the park down toward Shibuya station, looking over a copy of his family register.

People often had trouble reading Tatsushi's name, and the town hall receptionist was no exception:

"Eh? Where did the 'suke' go?"

Adding just one Chinese character to his name changed its reading to "Ryūnosuke." Otherwise, it was read simply as "Tatsushi," a far less common one. The receptionist could hardly have been over twenty, and even before Tatsushi finished explaining to her that he was now the head of the family, the freckles on her unmade-up face disappeared in a sea of red when she realized her mistake: Ryūnosuke was his father's name.

The object of his discontent was the large X over that very name. Though it simply marked that person as deceased, it seemed to deny the notion of existence altogether. Either way, it made him uneasy.

The air conditioning in the town hall had been turned up much too high for his liking. Sitting in his sweat-soaked polo shirt, he caught a slight chill by the time his name was called. Only when he received his copy of the register and went back outside did he find relief in the gradual warmth that enveloped him. Said relief proved fleeting, as sweat resumed its flow and weariness took over.

Being on a hill gave him a panoramic view of the city: a collage of people, cars, and ocean. Though summer was in its death throes, the afternoon sun was relentless. Everything from the roofs of parked cars to the hair of passersby flared into wisps of light. Heat mirages shimmered on the asphalt of distant streets.

He paused for a moment, having no interest in diving into that roiling ocean. He blinked into the glare and continued on.

From Shibuya, he took the Tokyo–Yokohama line and got out at Jiyūgaoka, where he transferred to the Ōimachi. Three stops later, he arrived at Todoroki. A five-minute walk from Todoroki station brought him to Ritsuzen-ji, a Shingon Buddhist site that had long served as his father's family temple.

He was there to obtain the death register kept in its care. He gave his name at the rectory and was led into the guestroom. Even without air conditioning, the temple's interior was refreshingly cool against the persistent heat outside its walls.

Five minutes passed before the chief priest presented himself.

"Sorry to keep you waiting."

The priest was only Tatsushi's age and had decided to enter the priesthood after graduating with a literature degree from Keiō University. Having only caught the occasional glimpse of him in the inner temple, Tatsushi was a bit nonplussed to find the priest in his "working" attire of T-shirt, jeans, and traditional sandals.

"I'm terribly sorry for the long absence," Tatsushi said, rising halfway from his seat.

The priest motioned for him to sit back down as he unburdened himself opposite him.

"Mr. Kōki's grave is always so immaculate. It appears someone has been coming to pay respects."

"Is that so?"

While this was only natural, Tatsushi couldn't help but be surprised. He went through a mental list of anyone who might come to visit his father's grave. He himself hadn't been there in almost two years.

"So, about the death register . . ."

"Yes, I have it here."

The priest offered a small bundle wrapped in silk.

"May I?" said Tatsushi, cutting it open and taking out the book inside.

It was bound in a black wooden cover that was rough to the touch and crumbled even as he opened it. The browned paper was brittle from age and gave off a distinct aroma. It had the look of dead leaves and was still bellowed together.

He carefully turned a page, revealing the words *Death Register Prepared by Tomoto Kōki on This the Seventh Month of 1942* written in ebony ink.

"He had remarkably nice handwriting, didn't he?"

Tomoto was Tatsushi's grandfather, and he saw no reason for this priest to know anything about a grandfather even *he* hardly remembered. Tatsushi looked up at the priest, who was now smiling. He now thought it strange that they were the same age.

The priest offered his blessings and stood up.

"Have you visited the grave already?" he asked.

"No, I'm going there now."

"Right, then. I bid you well."

He offered a ceremonious bow. Tatsushi returned the gesture, his head swirling with a rush of blood. At that moment, he felt oddly ignorant.

Exiting the room, he found the outside world just as scorching as when he left it. He stepped across the rough gravel and went around to the nave, continuing up a flight of stone steps into the graveyard.

The Kōki family site was the innermost of three plots, the other two as yet unpopulated by gravestones. He crouched down in front of the grave. Cicadas buzzed noisily amid a tangle of branches high overhead, their shrill voices phasing into a dissonant drone.

"So this was my father," he said inwardly, if only to confirm what he was seeing.

The priest was right. Someone had been here not too long ago and left a bundle of white chrysanthemums, vibrant and firm despite the heat, in offering. The incense ashes were still fresh.

Tatsushi rose to his feet and wiped his forehead with the back of his hand, his body immobilized by the unpleasant symphony of insects.

It began with a dream he had while crashing at a friend's place after a long night of drinking. That had been a month ago, but even now when he closed his eyes he could see the ocean's bright surface and the dusty ground burning in the sun.

At first, he saw himself in the boy, in light of the fact that Katō-sensei, a.k.a. "Mr. Dracula," had been his homeroom teacher in elementary school. The sensation of the wind blowing past his cheeks as he sped along on his bicycle was also reminiscent of his own childhood.

But somewhere along the way, the boy changed into his father—had, in fact, always been his father.

When he awoke, his throat was painfully dry, and that feeling of hopelessness was a long time in leaving him.

He was still in high school when his father died, over a decade ago. Thinking back on his father's death filled his heart with regret.

—*That man was like a flower in the desert.*

His mother once told him this when he asked about his father.

—*But then the rainy season comes, you see. The rain begins to pour down and that tender bud bursts into bloom. A most beautiful flower indeed.*

He had difficulty grasping his mother's analogy at the time. Sure, his father had died at the tender age of forty-two, but he didn't see how that made him a flower.

Only now did he understand.

When he was still in his twenties, Tatsushi's father founded an educational publishing company called Riu Press. By the time Tatsushi was sixteen, the company had gone under.

Riu Press showed great promise in its first ten years of business, during which it churned out several highly regarded publications and was hailed as the "next big thing" in the industry. Looking back on it now, Tatsushi could see that such praise had been well earned.

At a time when encyclopedias were only indexed according to the cumbersome Japanese syllabary, Riu Press was the first to market a more user-friendly series tailored for elementary and middle school students. Ryūnosuke put his heart and soul into everything he made.

After this period of steady growth, Riu Press expanded its vision. With the backing of a leading supermarket corporation, they began setting up cram schools across the country. That was the beginning of the end.

The supermarket chain had climbed its way to the top with small profits and quick returns, though not without garnering accusations of aggressive sales tactics, peddling teaching materials door to door. And so, when Riu Press announced its new alliance, the company was unanimously attacked in the papers.

The press pulled no punches. Tatsushi could still see the headlines: *Cram Schools or Sham Schools?*

Just like that, "education" had been reduced to a moneymaking scheme, or so the press would have it seem by painting a distorted image far removed from what his father was trying to accomplish.

Everyone goes through rough patches in life. This was his father's. Though Ryūnosuke lent little credence to the slander, his prestigious new partners annulled their contract not even a month before the opening of their first school.

Riu Press had amassed a fair amount of credit sales, but Ryūnosuke refused to let this hinder the school's opening. It was his brainchild, after all. He filed a lawsuit against the corporation, but by then the company was in the red and employees were quitting left and right.

He made every effort to raise funds, but their financial plans had revolved around the supermarket's investments from the very beginning. Despite Ryūnosuke's persistence, Riu Press went bankrupt before the first trial.

But nothing would prepare Tatsushi for what followed.

Riu Press folded with an enormous debt hanging over its heads. Someone must have gotten wind of this, as the very next day a group of so-called cash-and-carry wholesalers came not only to the company but also to their home in Setagaya. Tatsushi had been playing messenger that day, delivering documents to the company, and was stunned at what he saw inside.

Everything was gone. Every piece of office equipment, from the furniture to the copy machines, had been confiscated. Tatsushi stood there in that cavernous space.

The wholesalers had a certain panache that Tatsushi had never witnessed before and which led him to pursue his current line of work.

His father died less than a year later from a heart attack.

That his mother likened her husband to a "flower in the desert" spoke of the intensity with which he lived. Ryūnosuke had started with a seed and watered it into a solid business, only to watch it wither away all too soon. The simile was almost too precise.

Ryūnosuke's assets were modest at best, though he had left some life insurance to fall back on. Tatsushi's mother stretched her savings to raise him and his sister, Shigeko, on her own, even managing to put him through college.

He started his first business while still a student. At that time, and perhaps even now, the sheer tenacity of the cash-and-carry wholesalers had made an indelible impression on his young mind. Reducing excessive distribution while lowering prime costs allowed him to sell everything at prices far lower than his competitors.

This happened to take place when a slew of fresh-faced young coeds on television were making it big. The public imagination had clearly set its sights on the college student demographic, making it the ideal marketplace. Students had ample leisure time and money to spend. Those three magic words, "brand-name merchandise," filled him with excitement.

At a time when falling premiums had shut out most European makers, he could take advantage of the cheaper open market percentage rates in Hong Kong. He spent a good year establishing an independent distribution route to sell these products through catalogs. Sales exceeded his expectations.

The year he graduated from college, he withdrew his independent business license and set up a stock venture before turning his efforts to discount airline tickets. With his entrenchment in the student demographic, all he needed was to procure cheap tickets in bulk and they were as good as sold.

After laying successful groundwork with brand merchandising and overseas tour packages, Tatsushi moved on to household appliances and fine china. Since he had stocked up on brand merchandise from cash-and-carriers who auctioned off wholesale lots from bankrupt corporations, he was able to cut back the buying cost to a mere fraction. Selling directly to consumers via catalogs yielded a huge profit margin.

On the whole, his company developed nicely. Shigeko began working, too, by which time her and their mother's economic hardships receded. Once secure, he paid off his own debts in full.

Looking back, he remembered only working, sustained by that memory from ten years ago. In all that time, he told himself he could be successful, too. He realized that he always had this passion, that it made him who he was.

Three months ago, a check put up by one of his trusted brokers bounced. Because they were long-standing clients, this came as quite a shock. He had planned to do mail order service in conjunction with a new precious metals manufacturer, but didn't have the necessary capital on hand. He considered explaining the situation to them, but was hesitant to show weakness.

Seeing that recovery would be a long time coming, he got some quick cash by selling his car and mortgaging his apartment, which still had unpaid loans. Raising funds nevertheless proved to be an arduous task, and for added pressure the precious metals manufacturer was anxious to put its plan into action.

Whatever percentage he could collect would be fine with him. Not that everything had been smooth sailing. He had made it this far by seizing opportunities whenever and wherever they arose.

It bogged him down completely. He saw and thought about nothing else, and whenever he did have a free day, he filled the

void with alcohol. It was through a haze of inebriation that Tatsushi had had the dream.

Which was why the boy's yearning coincided so strangely with
his own. Still, he sensed it was his father.

He hardly knew anything about his father's childhood.
Ryūnosuke's past never concerned him when he was alive, much
less after his passing, but had been gnawing at his heart in the wake
of that dream. If only he could find out more, then he would know
for sure if the boy in his dream was indeed his father.

After leaving Ritsuzen-ji behind for Jiyūgaoka, he transferred to
a Yokohama-bound train. Upon reaching the city, he got off at the
third stop, and from there took a fifteen-minute bus ride to see his
mother and sister.

As he was walking through the small shopping district near the
bus station, he heard a familiar voice behind him:

"No way . . . it *is* you."

Shigeko came running up to him in sandals, her arms burdened
with plastic shopping bags.

"Fancy meeting you here. It's been a long time."

"It has. I should stop by more often. So, how's the company?"

"I quit last month."

"Really? Why?"

Shigeko furrowed her brow and slowly looked up to her younger
brother's face.

"I'm getting married. Forgotten already?"

Tatsushi felt the blood drain from his head. He had been so occupied with work that the most important moment in his sister's
life had totally slipped his mind. She was to wed at the end of No-
vember.

"Ah, that's right," he muttered vaguely.

His sister faltered, but smiled all the same.

"How's mom?" he said by way of changing the subject.

"Oh, good, good. She's been worried about you, though."

"Why's that?"

Tatsushi's voice grew firm despite himself. He hadn't told his mother or his sister about his current predicament. Shigeko was somewhat puzzled by her brother's forceful tone.

"Why, you ask? We don't hear much from you these days, and you hardly ever pick up when we call."

"Oh . . . is that all?"

He breathed a sigh of relief. He felt useless.

Since getting his company off the ground, he had left Yokohama to live on his own and could count the number of times he had gone back on one hand.

With his business on track and Shigeko's new job secured, he had managed to alleviate their economic burdens, but his absence from home had been the one debt he couldn't seem to clear. While part of him was eager to get to know his father's background, another part of him refused to empathize.

He hadn't seen the apartment in ten years. He remembered when it first went up, but now saw a weathered shell of its former self as the familiar white walls came into view.

He stood in front of the elevator and pressed the button.

"Say, you didn't drive here, did you?" said Shigeko, only now thinking to ask.

"Uh, no," he answered distantly as they got on the elevator. Thankfully, his sister didn't press him further on the matter.

"I'm home!" she proclaimed as she flung open the door.

"Welcome back," came a voice from inside.

"You'll never guess who I bumped into."

Shigeko grinned, turning to her brother with a finger to her lips. She rustled up a pair of slippers and offered them to him.

"Who's that?" their mother asked, not bothering to get up. Tatsushi and Shigeko entered to find her reclining in the sitting room reading a newspaper.

After noticing they had a guest, she looked up to see her son's face. She jumped to her feet, unable to hide her surprise. Shigeko smiled with amusement at her mother's reaction before going straight into the kitchen to prepare tea.

"Sorry I haven't kept in touch," Tatsushi said, taking a seat at the dining table.

His mother joined him and began barraging him with questions.

"You'd better be, young man. It's not like you live *that* far away. Anyway, enough of that. How are things? How's business coming along?"

"I went to see the priest. The grave is being kept up nicely. Someone's been visiting."

"That would be me."

"Eh?"

"I make it a point to go once every month. That's why it looks so nice. I was there just last week."

"Oh, I see."

"I'm assuming you've never taken the time?"

"I have, as a matter of fact."

Shigeko finished with the tea and carried it inside, taking a seat beside her brother.

"But why now, all of a sudden?"

"Well, about that . . ."

After a moment's hesitation, he took out the death register.

"What's that?," asked Shigeko.

"I did some digging, and was told the temple would have it. I wanted to see it for myself."

"Oh my," his mother whispered as she began flipping through it. He, too, shared her admiration for the paper's age and the austerity of its handwritten characters.

Thirteen names were recorded in the register. Among them were four without the surname Kōki. The oldest year of death was entered as June 5, 1901. In accordance with Buddhist tradition, a posthumous title was recorded along with the given name: *Shin'ichi Kōki, Died age 3.* Below that in small parentheses was written: *eldest brother.*

Shigeko stared at the death register for a long time, sighing with wonder.

"Who made this?"

"Grandpa, I should think. Look, it's written right here: Tomoto Kōki."

"So it is."

Shigeko was half-absorbed, delicately tracing the characters with her fingers:

September 15, 1913

Ei Kōki

Died age 31 (mother)

August 20, 1926

Shintarō Kōki

Died age 50 (father)

Shigeko's fingers stopped at these entries.

"These must be our great-grandparents on grandpa's side. Shintarō and Ei. I never even knew their names."

Tatsushi and his mother were practically beside themselves as they followed Shigeko's fingers. The frontispiece indicated July 1942, but there were deaths recorded after, so their grandfather had presumably drawn up the register that very year, making record of every death in the family since.

Shigeko jumped from one name to another.

"What's this?" she said suddenly, looking at her mother and brother almost with scrutiny. "Mom, who's this Otojirō Nishihara?"

"Which one, now?"

Their mother brought her eyes closer to the paper. Tatsushi had noticed before Shigeko even pointed to it. He was positive there was no one with that surname among his relatives. But there it was: *Otojirō Nishihara, Died age 72 (father)*.

"Grandpa's father was Shintarō, right? Maybe this Nishihara was our nana's father?"

Their mother shook her head.

"Impossible."

"Why?"

"Because your nana remarried in 1951. Maybe he just put it down in the register."

"Yeah, makes sense."

Neither Tatsushi nor Shigeko had seen their grandmother since the funeral, but Katsuko was alive and well. She had divorced Tomoto right after the war and was now remarried under the surname Ueda.

Since she and her second husband had no children together, Tatsushi's father had taken him to his grandmother's house in Shinagawa on many occasions when he was a boy. He remembered calling Katsuko's husband "Grampy Ueda." Since his father's death, he had grown estranged from that side of the family.

He didn't know the details of his grandparents' divorce, but had heard talk of Tomoto having a mistress.

"Does that mean Nishihara was grandpa's new wife's father?" Shigeko ventured.

Their mother shook her head again.

"I've no idea. But to make her way into the register . . ."

"If *you* don't know, mom, then who does?" asked the two siblings in unison. Their mother pursed her lips and eyed them both.

"I'm not sure," she said by way of excuse. "Just because your father and I were married doesn't mean we grew up together. And besides, by the time we got together, Katsuko was living with Ueda. Even had I wanted to find out, there was no one left to ask. At any rate," she added, "the Kōki family has never been without its share of drama, so I never saw fit to pry."

"Hmm." Tatsushi rubbed his nose. Something wasn't sitting right with him. "Oh well."

His mother pouted.

"Then who was dad raised by?" Tatsushi asked.

"I really couldn't say. Your father was already living on his own when we first met. But I know that he graduated high school in Kyushu, so he was in Kyushu until then at least."

"But wasn't his permanent residence in Shibuya? He was the patron of a temple in Tokyo. It was always Tokyo."

"Yes, that was my understanding. Your father's father, well, let's see . . . that would be Shintarō, yes? I heard he was a sake dealer in Shibuya."

"A sake dealer? I never knew that. But then, why did dad go to high school in Kyushu?"

"I guess he was left in someone else's care."

"Yes, but left to whom?"

"How should I know?" their mother said, throwing up her hands. She was clearly uncomfortable with the direction this conversation was taking.

"But Katsuko married Ueda and lived with him in Shinagawa. So where was Tomoto all that time? Don't you know, mom?"

"I don't know about that . . . but when I came to Tokyo to be with your father, your grandfather just showed up out of nowhere."

"'Out of nowhere?' What's *that* supposed to mean?"

"Exactly what it sounds like. He came by the house quite frequently before he passed on. Don't you remember?"

"No, I don't. How old do you think I was?"

Even as Tatsushi and his mother bickered over the past, Shigeko continued flipping through the death register with deep interest.

"Hey, you two," she interrupted, tapping her brother on the shoulder.

"What is it?"

"Look at this. Notice anything?"

They followed her finger:

February 2, 1962 1:32 am

Tomoto Kōki

Died age 60

That the date of his death had been recorded down to the exact time and that below his age there was no mention of family relation set this entry apart from the others. Because all genealogical information had been recorded in relation to Tomoto thus far, there was no way he could have written it. The penmanship was clearly different.

The three of them stared at the ebony-inked characters. It was as plain as day.

"That's *dad's* handwriting," said Shigeko, breaking the silence.

"I didn't even know this existed. When would he have written this, I wonder?"

Their mother seemed genuinely surprised. This meant that their father had also taken it out of the temple, where he returned it after Tomoto's death.

Tatsushi couldn't help but wonder how it must have felt for his father to record the Buddhist name of his *own* father.

"Well, if it isn't little Tatsuo from next door," the wide-eyed woman said. She was livelier than Tatsushi had imagined.

Just when he thought the family death register would divulge no clues about his father's childhood, Tatsushi had suddenly remembered the old woman who lived next door to them in Setagaya.

He and Shigeko used to call her the "old lady out back" when they were kids, so he always had an image in his mind of someone elderly. For all he knew, she might already be dead. But now that he had gone to see her, she didn't look a day older than seventy, which meant she was probably only in her fifties back then.

"My, how you've grown," she said, taken aback by her unexpected guest.

Tatsushi had to smile at the fact that she was speaking like that to someone in his thirties. He and Shigeko used to play at her house often, and it seemed the "old lady out back" still saw him as that same little boy.

The house where he originally grew up had been torn down to make way for a new building. Despite being surrounded by a crisscross of private railway tracks, it was far from any station, and except for a few business districts, one could still see long stretches of land dotted with rickety wooden houses. There were even fields a little farther in. But ever since the subways began carving their way through some years back, the terrain had changed completely.

"I wanted to ask you about my father," he said, wasting no time in broaching the subject.

She looked up at him with a start.

"Ryūnosuke?"

"Yes. When my father was little, I understand he lived with my grandparents."

"Ah, he did indeed. But he was taken away before he started middle school."

"Taken away?"

"Mm hm."

"By whom?"

She hesitated, averting her eyes in silence.

Tatsushi steadied himself.

"My father is dead."

She turned to him perplexedly.

"It was a long time ago, I was still in high school."

She inhaled, then exhaled like a gale of wind.

"Is that so?" she muttered.

"It wasn't until then that I realized how little I knew about my father. I've resolved myself to find out more about him."

At this, she sniffled, her hunched shoulders trembling slightly.

"Your grandfather's house was destroyed in the air raids," she began cautiously, still avoiding his gaze.

Tomoto had been in Manchuria during the war. Katsuko and Ryūnosuke stayed behind in Japan to hold down the fort, as it were. She couldn't recall the exact year Tomoto was to depart for the front, but in either event, Tatsushi's father, she said, was "just a boy" at the time.

The air raids intensified and the house was destroyed in the final year of the war. Katsuko took her son and sought temporary asylum elsewhere. The war ended soon thereafter, at which time she came back here, waiting for Tomoto's return in the most meager of shelters. Her story of hardship was one of many.

"We packed ourselves like sardines in these shacks, seven to a unit."

But Tomoto never came back. Ryūnosuke was already moving on to elementary school and Katsuko barely eked by.

"Most people in those days had to sell off their possessions just to survive . . . but she lost everything she held dear. Those were hard times. She couldn't even be sure of having enough rice for tomorrow."

The old woman took a breath and stared at her wrinkled, terra cotta hands.

Katsuko continued to wait for her husband's return. In the year following the war, after much anxious waiting, she finally received word from him. The news wasn't good.

"Tomoto had already been in Kyushu right after the war, but . . ."

". . . with another woman?" Tatsushi finished for her.

She shot a glance back at him and searched his face.

"Exactly," she continued. "If I remember correctly, I think her name was Masa."

"Masa . . ."

Katsuko had been thrown to the wayside with no say in the matter. As if that weren't enough, she had been forced to hand over Ryūnosuke, her only son.

Tatsushi massaged his forehead as he pictured a young boy crying himself hoarse over this traumatic separation.

"Things were different then. Women just didn't speak out in those days. There was nothing she could do."

"So that's how my father ended up in Kyushu?"

That explained why his father had graduated from high school there. It all made sense now. Until Ryūnosuke finished school, he lived with Tomoto and his new love interest.

She nodded silently to Tatsushi's question. He pressed her for more.

"And when did my father return to Tokyo?"

"Hmm . . . that must have been in 1955. Around the time he was accepted into university."

"Was he alone?"

"Yes." Again, she hesitated, but not before immediately relenting. "If you ask me, I think he came to Tokyo with the intention of living with his mother."

"Is that so?"

"It seems Ryūnosuke didn't know that Katsuko had remarried."

Tatsushi went silent for a moment.

So his father came to Tokyo to see his mother, from whom he had been forcibly snatched away, only to be met with more despair.

"Such a shame, really," she said, her eyes growing distant.

"But didn't my grandfather always come to visit when I was a baby? When did he come to Tokyo?"

"Let's see. It would've been after Ryūnosuke set up house here. He built that place with his own two hands, you know, and Tomoto had the nerve to barge in whenever he felt like it."

"Then where was my grandfather living at that time?"

"I heard he was in Wakabayashi."

Tatsushi expressed his gratitude and left his former neighbor behind.

Little by little, Ryūnosuke's past was coming into focus. It was anything but a happy one. Tatsushi walked the streets, feeling a heavy knot in his chest, even as another was unraveling.

Hearing about Wakabayashi reminded him of something.

After Ryūnosuke's death, he hardly had any contact with the Kōki side of the family, but in its heyday nearly everyone came to visit the Setagaya house for New Year's and other special occasions. Among them was a woman known as "Aunt Fumiko."

She always had her son in tow, the boy a few years Tatsushi's senior. Apparently, Fumiko had no husband. Whether because she was separated or widowed was never made clear. Tatsushi remembered her son, "Kazu-chan."

Aunt Fumiko and the boy were always on the quiet side, hovering in the background so that one hardly noticed when they came or left. In spite of the nickname, Tatsushi was certain his father had no sisters.

If Tomoto had indeed settled down in Wakabayashi after returning from Manchuria with this Masa, Fumiko had to be a relation of hers.

Tatsushi phoned his mother as soon as he got home. She berated him for suddenly pestering her all the time after such a long dry spell of communication.

"Did I have an aunt in Wakabayashi?"

The question caught her off guard.

"She used to come visit all the time when I was a kid. She had a son with her named Kazuhiko, or maybe Kazuo. I used to call him Kazu-chan for short."

"Oh, you mean Fumiko."

"Yes, Fumiko, that's her."

"What about her?"

"Was she on dad's side of the family?"

"You know I have no relatives in Tokyo."

"How was she related exactly?"

"Well, I can only assume she was your grandfather's niece."

"Tomoto's you mean?"

"Yes. But I can't say for sure."

"Why not?"

"Because it wasn't something to be discussed. Don't hold the past against me," his mother said, raising her voice a little.

Tatsushi smiled bitterly to himself.

"I'm not holding anything against you."

He asked her whether Fumiko still lived in Wakabayashi. His mother didn't know if Fumiko still lived where she used to, but if she did . . .

"Where was that?"

"Let me think. I believe it was called Shitanoya, or Kaminoya, something like that. It was a row-housing commune."

"Row-housing?"

"Barracks left over from the war. There was a cluster of about ten of them."

"So that's where Fumiko lived?"

"Yes, with her son. I don't think Shitanoya was its official name, though."

It took some finagling to get the location out of her, as she had only visited the place twice or so. It was so long ago and her memory was hazy, but Tatsushi got as many details as he could and hung up the phone.

Just as he was making up his mind to go the next day, provided he could set aside the time, the phone rang.

It was his associate, Awata.

"Just got a call from Ezaki at Darts."

Darts was a partner company that had also fallen victim to bounced checks.

"And what did he have to say?"

"Ezaki has taken it upon himself to organize the creditor hearings. Everything hits the fan at eleven tomorrow, Toranomon City Hall. Seeing as you don't have much on your plate, I took the liberty of telling them you'd be there as well."

"All right."

Tatsushi's company had only a handful of employees. The office was small; their annual turnover anything but. Apart from Tatsushi, everyone who worked there was in their twenties. Awata was different in that Tatsushi mentored him in college. Awata had only been with them for two years, but saw everything on Tatsushi's level.

"What is it?" Awata asked, noting the depression in Tatsushi's voice.

"Oh, it's nothing. Is that all Ezaki had to say?"

"Yes, he said the formation of the committee all depends on how things go down tomorrow."

"Got it."

Knowing that Ezaki was involved, it was likely that Tatsushi would have a part to play once it came down to getting the hearing committee together.

Tatsushi hung up the phone and let out a breath of stale air from deep within his lungs. It seemed his excursion would have to wait.

One week later, he finally made it to Wakabayashi.

After looking up Shitanoya and Kaminoya on a map, he wasn't surprised to find no town by either name in the vicinity. Whether due to his mother's weak memory or because the past twenty years had seen recognizable landmarks all but destroyed, he nevertheless stumbled upon a broad street.

There he discovered a two-level crossing, sandwiched between a bus switchyard and a large building, which resolved into an overpass.

The commune was likely long gone. And on the off chance he did find it, there was no guarantee that Fumiko would be there.

He stood at the crossing and lit a cigarette. Half of him wanted to turn back and leave. He would have done just that if not for the small police depot he spotted at the end of the overpass.

He tossed his cigarette onto the asphalt and snuffed it out with his shoe before hurrying over.

"Excuse me, I'd like to ask you something."

A young officer sat in a folding chair at a steel desk. He glanced up from beneath the brim of his navy-blue cap.

"I was hoping you could tell me where I might find a Shitanoya or Kaminoya in the area."

"Huh?"

The officer uncrossed his legs and put his hands on his thighs.

"Is that a surname?"

"No, not at all."

"The name of a town?"

"No, not exactly. It would have been the nickname of a street."

"Beats me."

The officer shook his head, laughing with a hint of derision. This was going nowhere. Just then, a senior officer poked his head out of the back-room door.

"I think you mean Uenoya."

"What?"

"It was Uenoya. No one uses that name anymore. You know how these things change. The locals called it Uenoya for a good while after the war."

The officer emerged, scratching a head of graying hair.

Tatsushi's heart was in his mouth.

"Does it still exist?"

The man laughed with an amusement befitting of his years.

"Sure does. Under a different name, of course."

"No, I mean the row-housing."

"Row-housing, you say?"

"Yes, I heard there was some kind of commune."

"Oh, that." He laughed again. "The barracks, you mean. Now that you mention it, I do remember them." He looked up suddenly. "Are you looking for someone?"

"Well, I . . ." Tatsushi hesitated, but decided it was best to be honest. "I'm looking for a relative."

"Who?"

"That's just it . . . I only know her first name: Fumiko."

The senior officer scanned the housing chart with his fingertip. He smiled and shook his head.

"Not much help without a last name."

"I see."

Tatsushi left immediately, with only directions to go on.

These he followed, making a mental picture of the map at the station. The "town" of Uenoya amounted to little more than a small lot.

As he dodged the elementary school students rushing back home, a narrow path came into view, running behind the telephone poles at the village dump. Here the pavement ended, giving way to a dirt road blanketed in pebbles. Deep green weeds grew thickly on either side of the path. This had to be it.

It was a wonder such a place still existed in the Tokyo metropolitan area. Barracks housing was a thing of the past, but this rare cluster had stood the test of time. Tatsushi started down the path with renewed confidence.

Despite a stillness in the air, he heard chimes somewhere up ahead. He followed the sound to a brown painted fence. A cat yawned in the gap below. There was a similar fence at the neighboring house. White linens billowed in the wind.

Someone stepped out of the second house. Tatsushi could only make out her faded hair and scrawny legs.

He made his way around to a frail wooden side gate that had been left open.

"Excuse me."

The woman turned around sluggishly. Her straw-like hair was tied loosely behind her back. A few ragged strands tangled about the nape of her powdery dry neck.

"Um . . . Aunt Fumiko?"

The reserved woman of memory had grown old and ragged, but her composure and narrow eyes betrayed the disguise of her age.

"Yes . . . ?"

She knitted her eyebrows and nodded apprehensively.

"I'm, uh, Tatsushi Kōki. Ryūnosuke's son."

The moment he said that, her mouth dropped open and she stood there petrified. She let out a strange exclamation of surprise, then pursed her lips and stammered in search of something to say. She quickly rolled up the laundry she was holding, her actions tinged with shame, and invited him inside.

Tatsushi stepped into the small front yard, hardly believing that he had found her. From the deck he saw a single sitting area and a modest kitchenette, the only two rooms in the house. The sun beat down on the yard, where the damp soil was overrun with weeds. The house itself was poorly lit and dismal on the inside. Aside from a storage chest and a small television artlessly placed on the splintering floor mat, there was no furniture to speak of. Where the alcove would normally have been he saw a Buddhist altar, splendidly incongruous with its surroundings.

Fumiko climbed in from the deck.

"Please," she said, gesturing inside.

"Here's fine," he blurted out, sitting himself down on the sun-bathed deck.

The wind was still now and he could feel sweat sticking to the back of his neck. Though technically autumn, summer was refusing to leave.

At last, he managed to compose himself. He looked at Fumiko, who had her back to him.

"I'm sorry for showing up out of the blue like this. But seeing as I didn't know your phone number . . ."

He watched her fixing some refreshments in the kitchen. She was thin, though her calves were sagging.

"I never thought we'd meet like this."

Owing perhaps to her memories of Tatsushi, Fumiko seemed unfazed around him. He, on the other hand, knew nothing more than her face and name, and only her first name at that. Finding this place was worth the trouble.

The sound of running water trickled from the kitchen. In his mind: an image of Fumiko huddled secretly in a corner with her son. Though he imagined her to be no older than fifty, she was, in fact, pushing sixty.

Fumiko came back with a tray and a cup of barley tea. She placed the tray onto the deck and sat on the floor mat next to him. Instead of sitting in the normal fashion with her legs tucked under her, she plunked down on her bottom and stuck out her legs. It made Tatsushi somewhat uneasy. Sitting down, she was surprisingly short.

For someone who should have been flustered at this unexpected visit, Fumiko was calm and collected. Tatsushi felt like she saw right through him, ready for whatever he had to say.

"I know it's a bit rude for me to come here unannounced."

Tatsushi spoke despite his apprehension. Fumiko nodded, urging him on.

"So, you are . . . my grandfather's niece, yes? My father's cousin, in other words," he said by way of confirming his mother's convoluted genealogy.

What he really wanted to know was whether she had any connection to this woman known as Masa, his grandfather's lover. But he withheld the name for now.

Fumiko didn't answer and instead looked at him misty-eyed, her mouth agape. Tatsushi diverted his eyes.

"I . . ." she muttered after a pause.

"What is it?"

"It's just, well, you've already got it wrong," she answered, punctuating every word, her voice like a little girl's.

"Meaning what?"

"That's not who I am."

Tatsushi was silent.

"I'm nothing more than an acquaintance," she said, looking up suddenly.

"What?"

He felt like she was dodging the question, but reluctantly heard her out.

"I owe much to Tomoto," she said, as if to herself. Her speech grew distant.

Tatsushi had a feeling he wouldn't get much out of her even if he just asked her about Masa directly. Was it mere coincidence that she was in Wakabayashi during the time his grandfather lived there?

Tatsushi's hopes quickly faded, even as he became more relaxed.

He crossed his legs, resigned to not getting what he had come for.

"Your son, Kazu-chan was it? How is he?" he said as a gossiper might.

"He's married."

"Is he now? Makes sense, I suppose. He must be two or three years older than me."

"A Rooster."

"Come again?"

"Kazuya is a Rooster."

"Oh, his zodiac sign, you mean. That would make him three years older."

The more he talked with Fumiko, the more troubled he became. She was too young to be senile. But she certainly was eccentric.

Her unfocused gaze was striking and made her even more distinct. Tatsushi looked away before because those eyes were so unbecoming of her age. He imagined she was quite slender and beautiful in her day.

"You'll have to excuse me for dredging up the past like this. I'm sure it took you by surprise. Actually, I was just hoping to know a little more about my late father."

Only now did she perk up.

"What would you like to know?" she asked.

And yet, no matter what he wanted to ask, it was difficult to express notions that were hazy at best.

It was then that he thought of the death register at Ritsuzen-ji. He tried working it into the conversation as casually as possible.

"Aunt Fumiko, do you know an Otojirō Nishihara?"

"Nishihara . . ."

He saw a flash in the depths of her hollow eyes. Fumiko turned aside in the manner of a young lady and laughed through her nose.

"No, the only Nishihara I know is Masa."

This set off a crackle of fireworks in his head.

It made perfect sense now. Otojirō must be Masa's father. Though Tomoto never entered Masa's name into the register, since he had divorced Katsuko just for her, it was understandable that Tomoto had put down Otojirō's name as the father.

"You . . . knew Masa?"

"Knew her? She lived with Tomoto not a stone's throw away."

"She lived around here, then?"

"No."

"But you just said she lived . . ."

Tatsushi was growing more frustrated by the minute.

Fumiko laughed.

"No, no. That was in Sasebo, not Tokyo."

"Eh?!"

"Sasebo, in Nagasaki."

"Then you were also in Kyushu?"

The old woman went silent. She played with the hem of her skirt and gazed at the weeds out front, her mind elsewhere. There was something off about her.

At least the mystery of Otojirō Nishihara had been solved, but Tomoto's time in Wakabayashi was still fuzzy. This was good enough. At least this visit hadn't been a total waste.

"I see. Was Masa's last name Nishara?"

Silence.

"No? I only ask because there was a Nishihara recorded in my grandfather's death register."

Again, Fumiko turned away. Tatsushi then remembered her curious reaction when he first introduced himself.

"What happened after my father was in Kyushu?"

But Fumiko refused look at him, her lips sealed.

If she knew anything about his father when he was in Kyushu, he felt entitled to that information, but being in her presence was beginning to stifle him.

He knew it was time to go. He apologized once more for the intrusion. Just then, Fumiko said something.

Tatsushi turned around.

"Come again?"

Fumiko was sitting as she was before, lowering her head politely.

"I feel so sorry for him . . ."

He couldn't quite grasp the meaning of those words. Tatsushi acknowledged them curtly and left the way he came. He hadn't noticed it when he arrived, but there was a small plaque hanging next to the gate with characters written in black ink. Time had left it all but faded completely, and he couldn't make it out. It was then he realized he never asked for her last name.

Tatsushi walked along the narrow unpaved path, trying not to step on the sharper stones. The schoolchildren had already gone home. He came out onto the main road, red in the setting sun. The lingering heat was intense, but the streets waited for autumn with open arms.

Tatsushi stopped at the crossing, Fumiko's parting words ringing in his ears: *I feel so sorry for him . . .*

Why had she said that? Was it meant for his dead father?

He moved his feet again. He couldn't recall whether Fumiko and her son had attended his father's funeral. Either way, the timing of her condolences was unsettling.

The crossing sign began to blink. Tatsushi gave up and shuffled along, looking at the light as if it were some foreign object.

His heart pounded in his head. It struck an unpleasant chord inside him, phasing with the flashing in front of his eyes.

—*I owe much to Tomoto . . .*

Fumiko's cryptic words looped endlessly in his head.

With the creditor hearings at last under way, Tatsushi assisted Ezaki as mediator.

Though Ezaki was five years older than him, they were kindred spirits in that Ezaki had put together the Darts Company during his college days. Tatsushi was first introduced to Ezaki when starting his own company. Darts had managed his mail orders of imported furniture. For this and more, he was much indebted to Ezaki.

Ezaki knew the situation with Tatsushi's company inside and out, so he was the first person Tatsushi consulted when everything blew up in his face. But even Ezaki was scratching his head over this one.

"I'm stumped. A bounced check? The possibility never even crossed my mind."

It had been a while since he had seen Ezaki, who looked beat sitting there in the hotel tearoom. Everyone bore their fair share of this burden, Ezaki not least of all. One look at his clothing would have pegged him as a capable businessman, but the nails on his fingers, cradling a short unfiltered cigarette, had grown long with neglect.

Ezaki said it was best to suspend all further dealings with this precious metals wholesaler. The bankruptcy of the brokers in question involved the credit companies as well, a fact that served to drag the hearings on.

"Are you moving on to a new project?" Ezaki said.

"You bet I am. After all the progress we've made, we can't afford to waste time on this."

"I'm not saying you should start over. Just that you should hold out a bit longer."

"It's all the same to me. Won't make any difference."

Ezaki sighed with a puff of smoke. Even as he put out his cigarette in the ashtray, he was fumbling to light another.

The tearoom walls were glass-sided. Pristine white light poured in from outside, illuminating Ezaki's pockmarked cheeks. After lighting up a fresh cigarette, he squinted into the glare and went on.

"My hands are full. I shouldn't say any more."

Tatsushi looked up, waiting for the rest. Ezaki stared blankly at the hotel courtyard beyond the window. There was a parking lot past the garden. A sedan had just pulled in, out of which stepped a thirty-ish married couple.

The wife got out of the back seat. She had a light blue sweater slung across her shoulder and seemed a bit tense. She made for the hotel, not bothering to wait for her husband, who was taking his time. A moment later he turned around, spreading his arms wide.

A five-year-old girl clutching a teddy bear emerged with the woman and ran up to him. The man hugged his daughter and propped her up effortlessly onto his shoulders.

Lured in by Ezaki's interest, Tatsushi found himself also gazing vacantly at this scene. The two men came back to their senses and looked at each other. Tatsushi couldn't help but notice what an immense difference there was between these two worlds, separated by a mere pane of glass.

"Just . . . don't go overboard on this one."

With this, Ezaki finished off his cold coffee, grabbed the receipt, and walked over to the register.

Only then did it occur to Tatsushi that Ezaki had gotten divorced two years ago and had a wife and little girl of his own.

After they said goodbye and he started down the afternoon streets, Tatsushi felt his entire body wrapped in a haze of fatigue. He couldn't think straight, and it put a strain on his motivation.

His mind and body were practically dormant. He wanted nothing more than to wrap himself in cold sheets and sleep. The preparations for the hearings had left him with little time for respite. And despite being on his way home, an opportunity for rest was the last thing that awaited his return.

He contacted Awata first to run over particulars and draw up a list. This meant he would have to put Fumiko from his mind.

Once in his room, he flung open the window to the veranda, letting out the stale air that had accumulated in his absence. The weather had cooled in the past few days.

After putting in word to the company, he sat down at his computer, but made little headway. Perhaps it was because he had been out of the loop for so long that even the most trifling task seemed to take forever. It was already dark by the time he completed the first phase of his work.

Alone in his room, his empty stomach gurgled audibly, but even the prospect of eating seemed like a chore. He climbed into bed, gripped by an urge to stop anything and everything.

—*Want to know a secret, Tatsushi?*

His father's voice, back in middle school.

The threat of upcoming exams should have been his worst nightmare. Yet as one so focused, Tatsushi always made sure to be prepared. He studied alone his room, chained to his desk, and when being holed up in there became too much for him, took his study materials downstairs to the living room.

—*Ugh, I can't take any more of this.*

Tatsushi remembered throwing down his pencil, and what his father said:

—*Want to know a secret, Tatsushi?*

His father smiled.

—*That's when you stop.*

Tatsushi smiled bitterly at the ceiling. Of course, he would have stopped if he could, but his father knew all too well there were times when giving up wasn't an option. He still wasn't sure why his father told him this.

After so many days, fatigue had won over his hunger. He turned in bed, lulled into a deep sleep with the lights on.

By the next morning, he was at a breaking point. He stood in the kitchen, searching the refrigerator, only to find a pack of moldy cheese and a carton with about an inch of milk left at the bottom.

The bread in the cupboard appeared safe. And so, having no other choice, he fixed a meager breakfast of toast and coffee and fetched the morning paper.

Tatsushi took out the front section and business pages. Biting into his toast, he turned to the latter. At first, the bankruptcy scandal hadn't warranted enough attention to make its way into the gossip columns.

But in today's paper, Tatsushi couldn't help but notice the company's name headlining a full two-column article. Next to it, letters in gothic font read: *Associated Enterprises Heading for Bankruptcy.*

Tatsushi stared at the words and the toast fell from his hands. Darts had fallen victim to this same ripple effect.

Awata rang him just after eight o'clock.

"You heard?"

"Yeah, read it in this morning's paper."

"I'll be heading over to the Darts head office to gauge the situation."

"No, I'll go see Ezaki right away."

"Very well. I'll be back at the bureau office in the afternoon."

"Sounds good. I'll drop by later, then."

Tatsushi quickly changed his clothes and left, hailing a taxi outside.

Ever since Ezaki separated from his wife, he had been living alone in an apartment near Kōen-ji. The highway was jammed as usual. Tatsushi urged the driver to hurry. Seeing as rush hour was upon them, the driver insisted it didn't matter which way they took, but Tatsushi guided him through the back roads as best he could. Despite his persistence, it was almost ten o'clock by the time he arrived.

He slipped the driver a ¥10,000 note and got out of the car. He skipped the elevator and ran up the stairs, nearly tripping along the way.

He tried the doorbell, but there was no answer. He put his hand on the knob. It was unlocked. He stepped into a surge of stale air. It smelled just like Tatsushi's room the night before.

"Ezaki, are you in there?"

No answer. Ezaki was nowhere to be seen.

That left only the bedroom. Tatsushi opened the door to an immaculately made bed. He had a bad feeling about this. He approached the bedside closet and opened it, expecting the worst.

Empty. Where there should have been coats and suits, there was nothing.

Tatsushi supported himself on the knob, staring into the cavernous closet in disbelief.

Ezaki's disappearance immediately went public.

Any businessmen or company employees who had associations with him began hovering around his hometown of Hachiōji. At Tatsushi's request, Awata followed suit.

Even after the buzz died down, a few people were still hanging about, a handful of mobsters among them. Tatsushi recognized one familiar face among the crowd.

A woman felt his gaze upon her and turned around. Recognizing Tatsushi's face, she gave an expression of mixed emotions before nodding slightly. Ezaki's former wife.

"Hi . . ."

Tatsushi had no idea what to tell her. The woman turned away sharply and cut him off.

"You never listened to me."

She turned around and walked away with a click-clack of her heels.

Tatsushi deluded himself into thinking that those words were directed at him somehow, and he stared at her slender backside in shock.

He learned that Ezaki had returned home after their meeting at the hotel and vanished immediately thereafter. He remembered Ezaki's face in the sunlight, staring out at the family in the parking lot, his skin uneven, eyes bloodshot from the weariness of an un-stable life. Tatsushi could think of nothing else when he went to sleep. It made him want to scream. Where could Ezaki possibly be?

Once the Darts hype died down, he invited Awata over to his place to discuss a new plan of action. There was a mountain of problems in need of their prompt attention, not least of which was finding a replacement to preside over the creditor hearings.

Even the ever-composed Awata seemed bewildered about the Darts bankruptcy and Ezaki's subsequent disappearing act. Their talk dragged on past midnight. As Tatsushi was about to pour them some coffee, Awata hunched over with his narrow shoulders and did a rare thing by pointing to a bottle of scotch.

"Mind if I have a glass?"

Tatsushi felt a pang of guilt. Regardless of whether it was all an act, he knew it was up to the two of them to take the reins.

When they finally wrapped things up, it was just past one in the morning. Tatsushi dragged himself to his feet and called Awata a taxi.

As Awata was putting on his shoes, he turned around.

"Say, boss."

"Yes?"

"Aren't you scared?"

Tatsushi didn't know what to say. He could see Awata was des-perate.

After a moment, he tried to right himself.

"Don't be silly. Pull yourself together, man. We'll be fine."

He sent Awata off with a pat on the shoulder.

As Awata disappeared behind the door, Tatsushi felt like squat-ting down in resignation right then and there. Instead, he propped himself against the wall.

"You bet I'm scared," he said softly.

Not that anyone heard him. Still, it comforted him a little to admit it out loud.

He nestled himself into the living room sofa and grabbed the whisky bottle, pouring the remainder of its amber liquid into Awata's unfinished glass.

The alcohol stung his throat on its way down. Tatsushi rubbed his arms briskly.

He went back again to that fateful day at age sixteen, standing in his father's empty office and watching a truck speed away with all their possessions. It was the catalyst that set his life in motion.

He thought of his father. *You must've been scared, too*, he thought. Tatsushi wept cold tears.

He was never *not* scared. Despite his fears, he had moved up in the world. There was no turning back now.

He remembered what Ezaki's ex-wife had said: *You never listened to me.* It made him feel lonely.

In Tatsushi's eyes, the very thing that had enabled him to suppress this penetrating fear and move on was that single memory he kept going back to. Standing there in that cold, empty room, he had resolved to fill it with life.

He entrusted his body to the leather sofa. Since having that dream, he wanted to know about his father's history, if only to pinpoint the source of his perseverance.

Tatsushi could hardly tell if the tears falling down his cheek were even his. Feeling the droplets on the surface of his skin, he stared vacantly at the ceiling.

An opportunity came when he least expected it.

The creditor hearings continued to drag on, but Awata was beginning to recover from his temporary shock, and the exhaustion that had plagued everyone since the whole Darts debacle arose was finally clearing up. Even as Tatsushi found himself swamped, he felt his usual enthusiasm returning to him.

"A phone call for you, boss."

Tatsushi braced himself, as did with every phone call over the past few months.

"Who is it?"

"Says he's family."

Tatsushi drew a deep breath. His mother and sister rarely, if ever, called him at the office. He had told them not to. He spoke crossly without meaning to.

"Who is this?"

"Is this Tatsushi Kōki?" came a man's voice from the other end.

Tatsushi quickly changed his tone.

"Yes, this is he."

"I'm Kazuya. I take it you know who I am?"

Tatsushi fell silent. It took him a few moments to realize he was talking to Fumiko's son.

"Yes, uh, it's been a long time."

"I heard you went to see my mother."

He spoke curtly and in an accusatory manner. He sounded almost hostile.

"Indeed, I did."

Tatsushi was puzzled. Why had Kazuya taken such a sharp tone with him, despite having not spoken to one another in over ten years? And what reason did he have for calling Tatsushi in the first place?

"I'm upset that you would do this to me."

"Huh?"

"In any case, I would appreciate if you left my mother alone."

"I'm not sure I follow."

This brought only silence.

"Yes, I did meet with Aunt Fumiko, but I don't see what that has to do with . . ."

After a short pause, Kazuya heaved a sigh.

"You mean you don't know?"

"Know what?"

"I can't believe this."

"Please tell me. If not on the phone, then I'll make time to meet you in person."

Kazuya consented. They set a time and place and hung up.

"I thought you said it was a relative?" he said to the young receptionist who had connected his call.

She stared at Tatsushi's face blankly.

"But he said his last name was Kōki. I just assumed . . ."

"He did?"

He had an eye-opening thought.

"You're sure he said Kōki?"

"Positive."

Embarrassed, she raised a hand in apology. Tatsushi pressed his temples with his palms and stared at the top of the desk.

"Do you know what a 'flower cart' is?"

A plaintive ray of sunlight cast yellow patterns on the floor. The approaching dusk had weakened the sun's momentum, and the heat along with it. Autumn was here at long last.

"Flower cart?"

Tatsushi looked up suddenly, searching the face of the one before him.

"Yes, a flower cart."

Kazuya Kōki tried not to make more eye contact than was necessary, fixing his gaze instead on the mosaic of red and ochre splashed across the coffee shop floor.

As Tatsushi suspected, Tomoto had brought back a woman named Masa Nishihara with him from Manchuria to Sasebo.

Masa suffered from a violent disposition. Not long after beginning their new life in Sasebo, Tomoto spoke frequently of the son he had left back in Tokyo, and this planted a seed of uneasiness within her. She worried his yearning might make him go back. Apparently, it was never Tomoto's intention but rather Masa's firm demand that Ryūnosuke be brought over to Sasebo. Masa believed the child's presence would bond them.

"All of this I heard from my mother, so it might not be the full story," Kazuya added. "Masa was what they called a 'flower cart.' She ran a whorehouse in Manchuria. I can only assume that Sasebo was the kind of place where she could continue making a living. My mother was a prostitute."

To be sure, Tomoto had been promiscuous. His good nature and kindness overshadowed all other weaknesses. He wasn't the type to turn down anyone in need. Bringing Masa back from Manchuria was likely no more than a way of facilitating her return to Japan. When they arrived in Sasebo, however, Tomoto stayed with her longer than anticipated.

Fumiko had worked under Masa in Sasebo since she was seventeen, but during that time came to have relations with Tomoto. That was the year following the death of Masa's father, Otojirō Nishihara.

"Ryūnosuke even called her 'mother' once."

He must have understood the difference. When Ryūnosuke was first brought over, he constantly yearned for his real mother, but from middle school onward never mentioned Katsuko's name in front of Tomoto or Masa.

Even so, Ryūnosuke never thought of Masa as his mother. Given Masa's lack of maternal qualities, this was inevitable. When one day he did call her "mother," Masa told him flat out:

—No, I am not your mother.

Again, Tatsushi thought back to that boy in his mind crying himself hoarse at being separated from his real mother. And now that same boy stood before his father's mistress in shock, as if he had been smacked on the nose with the truth.

Tatsushi wrung his hands on his knees.

It wasn't long before Masa found out about Tomoto and Fumiko, and when she did, flew into a rage. She fired Fumiko and drove Tomoto out of the house. Despite the upheaval, she never considered giving up Ryūnosuke for a second. That was Masa's last will.

Ryūnosuke had no choice but to live with Masa Nishihara, a woman with whom he shared no blood or emotional ties, until he graduated from high school.

"I was born the year after my parents came to Tokyo. My father . . ."

Kazuya suddenly hesitated at that point in his story and searched Tatsushi's face for a moment. The man Kazuya knew as his father was Tatsushi's grandfather.

"My father died when I was about five or so, but after that my mother raised me, always saying, 'I feel so sorry for Ryūnosuke.'"

When Kazuya was born, Tomoto officially recorded Fumiko into the family register as his third wife. Fumiko's weak health often kept her bedridden after Kazuya's birth. Tomoto's frequent trips to see Ryūnosuke, who had just started his life in Tokyo, were a pretext to ask for money.

For as long as she was ill, this was okay.

Masa expanded her business interests and came to Tokyo. There she tracked down the house in Uenoya and made a surprise visit. Tomoto happened to be absent and Kazuya was too young to remember what happened. From that day on, Fumiko became mentally unstable. Though Fumiko was officially on record as his wife, her former status in Sasebo steered Ryūnosuke to live with Masa. Either way, Fumiko was much indebted to Tomoto for these various favors over the years.

No matter what Masa said or did to Fumiko when she visited Uenoya, it wasn't difficult to imagine that something in Fumiko withered away from that experience. She was still in the hospital when Tomoto died.

Ryūnosuke held his father father's funeral and protected Fumiko's existence so that even his mother didn't know who she was. When Fumiko was discharged, she witnessed the many hardships of parenthood firsthand. He had taken upon himself all the complications that had arisen because of Tomoto having relations with three successive women.

"That's why my mother has such a deep respect for Ryūnosuke."

Tatsushi was speechless.

"When I heard that you went to see my mother, I was surprised to find that I shared her feelings in that regard, but in her condition . . . I'm sorry if I was rude on the phone."

The sickness that had built a nest in Fumiko's heart over the years was revealing itself once again.

"He was old enough to be my father. But he was still my elder brother. Ryūnosuke was . . ." Kazuya stopped there and looked through the window.

Fallen leaves from the roadside trees spread along the crosswalk, kicked around by the feet of pedestrians.

Tatsushi looked up at Kazuya, urging him to go on. Seeing his profile, Tatsushi was overtaken by an unusual nostalgia.

"Ryūnosuke wasn't one to accept favors. He did everything in his power to help those around him."

"That he did."

"I can't really put it into words, but I almost feel like he did it to fill a gap inside him."

Tatsushi held his head and looked out the window in kind. He wanted to say something important, but didn't know what.

"He must've been lonely."

In the end, that was all he could come up with.

The only time his father ever lived a normal childhood was during those few years spent waiting for Tomoto's return at Katsuko's humble home. After that most unnatural period living with Masa Nishihara, it was only a matter of time before his father rushed back to Tokyo. But Katsuko had wasted no effort in creating a new home.

His father *was* lonely. And because of this, as Kazuya rightly put it, he did everything in his power for those around him.

What inspired his father was that very loneliness, so deeply rooted in him. No matter where he went, no matter where he ran, it was out of a need to escape that loneliness. But he still had to run.

"With Ryūnosuke gone, and my mom sick as she was, I was probably the only one who knew I was Ryūnosuke's younger brother by a different mother. Maybe it was never meant to be discussed."

"No," Tatsushi interrupted him mid-sentence. "I'm glad you told me."

Kazuya bowed his head in silence, then closed his eyes. He concealed his face a little. His Adam's apple moved up and down as he swallowed. He was choosing his words carefully.

He finally looked up and faced Tatsushi.

"I . . . um . . ."

"Yes?"

"I loved Ryūnosuke dearly."

A grumbling noise came from the pit of Tatsushi's stomach. He felt his throat tightening.

"Thank you very much," he said finally.

Even Tatsushi didn't know why he thanked him.

When he left the shop, the light had paled. The two men parted and went their separate ways.

After taking a few steps forward, Tatsushi suddenly realized something and turned around. Bathed in the orange flare of the setting sun, Kazuya looked like any other pedestrian among the urban bustle. But his back was weighted with all manner of thoughts, built up over the span of many years.

He remembered his condescension on the phone, which made him realize that living was never a simple matter, no matter who you were.

In much the same way Tatsushi's life began in that empty office as a boy of sixteen, at some point during his chaotic childhood Ryūnosuke had forged his own path.

He remembered it so clearly now, he wondered why he hadn't until then.

His father stood alone at the window in that vacant room. Upon noticing that Tatsushi had come in, he turned around.

—*Hey, son. Thanks for everything.*

His father was smiling. Yes, his father was smiling. Why was beyond him.

Tatsushi closed his eyes for a moment.

A long thin row of wooden planks on the water's surface; ripples in the canal sparkling like the bellies of upturned fish; that uneasy sensation of powerlessness as he stepped onto the first piece of wood.

It's not that he wasn't afraid, only that he couldn't save himself except by repressing his fears and moving forward.

Never knowing where the path led to, that constant threat of sinking to his death . . . what made his father go on? Was it simply the pressure of a loneliness that threatened to consume him? And if so, what was motivating Tatsushi now?

A steady stream of people were being swallowed by the subway entrance ahead. Tatsushi headed in their direction. As he blended into the crowd, he knew what his father had seen outside that window. It was all around him.

A Slender Back

Oisan passed away in the summer of Ryōji's twenty-second year.

Ryōji had been working in Tokyo since high school. When he received a phone call from the front desk, the early summer sun was at its peak, radiating with its triumphant power in the early afternoon.

"Are you Ryōji Nakata?" said an unfamiliar voice on the other end.

After confirming that he was, the man informed him that his father was dead.

At first, it didn't sink in.

"I see," he said, knowing what a foolish response it was even as he said it. He always likened his emotions to pomegranate seeds, and when Oisan's death finally hit him, he felt one of those seeds being audibly crushed inside him.

He thought back to when he was little, burning leaves in the front yard. He remembered consigning small insects to the crackling flames, and the faint squeal they made as their exoskeletons burst open.

His insides popped like one of those very insects, dying in whispered swan song. But even at this saddening news, he didn't say a word or shed a single tear. If there had ever been a time to cry over his death, he thought, it was then.

Ryōji said he would return home immediately and hung up the phone, only then realizing he had failed to identify the mystery caller.

Doubtless, Machiko had been there during his father's last moments, but under the circumstances would have been of little help. More likely, an obliging neighbor was managing the funeral and other arrangements.

Ryōji looked behind him to the customer waiting patiently in the barber's chair, draped from the neck down in a lavender sheet that gave her the appearance of some crude doll a child might make. She and the salon manager both stared at him like caged animals in a pet shop window.

He drew the manager aside and explained the situation. The manager's eyes went wide, less at the death of Ryōji's father than his lack of visible emotion, and recommended that he go straight home. Ryōji glanced at his customer and her still-wet hair and requested that be allowed to leave once he was finished with her.

As he repositioned himself behind her, the woman reached out a hand from beneath the plastic sheet and plucked out an issue from the stack of women's weekly circulars in front of the mirror.

"Something the matter, Ryōji?" asked the woman, a regular of his for the past several months.

"Nope, everything's fine."

He firmly grasped her wet hair, which looked as if it would make a rasping sound were he to rub it together. Having suffered the effects of many a dye job, it was heavily damaged, its natural color no longer discernible. Limp strands stuck to her head like seaweed, revealing the shape of her skull.

The woman looked up from her magazine and checked her reflection. Makeup caked her hollow cheeks. As she gazed into the mirror, which reflected truth more clearly than reality, Ryōji wondered what she might be feeling.

He pictured the discolored and uneven skin beneath her heavy foundation. The bags under her eyes were impossible to hide and said much about her daily life.

Just before she went back to her reading, their gazes met in the mirror. He smiled faintly at her reflection and the image responded, happier than his. He noticed the red lipstick stuck to her front teeth.

He held her hair in his left hand, dexterously snipping away with his right. The liberated strands fell into a pile, looking more frayed than they were on her head, reminding him of sawdust scattered on subway station stairways.

Her frame was dreadfully thin—so thin, she was practically two-dimensional—striking a curious balance with her diminutive, withered face. Her narrow shoulders prompted a sudden flashback.

—*There's something forlorn about our hair, isn't there, Ryōji.*

Machiko's voice echoed in his ears.

He felt as if his body had been beaten into submission. He sighed and looked out the window. The sun was as intense as ever, turning the other buildings into silver.

He returned to the apartment he had been renting for the last four years, only to find Atsuko lounging in the living room. The curtains were closed, lending the room a dark and depressing air. She turned to face him as he stepped through the door.

"What brings you home so early? Something up?" she said.

"I should ask you the same thing. Aren't you supposed to be working today?"

"Taking a paid holiday."

"What for?"

Atsuko worked for an eyeglasses chain. She was older than him by a year, and they had known each other for just as long. They didn't technically live together, but for the past six months she had been crashing at his place once or twice a week.

Ryōji was somewhat uncomfortable about the fact that she was still wearing the pajamas she borrowed from him the night before. He deliberately avoided looking in her direction, lest she detect his annoyance. He couldn't care less why she was taking a day off.

He slipped past her and undressed, going over bullet train schedules in his head. Atsuko observed his every move.

"And not just for today, either," she said as she watched him changing.

"Huh?"

"My day off."

"What do you mean?"

He tried to let it go, but his stomach was beginning to churn with irritation.

"Tomorrow, the day after . . ."

"What? Why?"

After a long silence, she replied, "There's something I've been meaning to talk to you about."

Ryōji finished changing and turned to her. Leaning on one arm, Atsuko was looking at her folded knees.

"Uh, sorry, but I . . ."

She lifted her head slightly.

". . . need to take a trip out to my hometown in the country now."

Atsuko drew in a deep breath, her cheeks sagging, not taking her eyes off him.

"When you say 'now,' you mean *right* now?"

"Yeah."

"What's wrong? Did something come up?"

"Actually, it's my father. He . . ."

Her eyes pressed for more.

"He collapsed."

"He's sick?"

"Yes . . . well, no. He's dead."

Atsuko gasped.

"Why didn't you tell me sooner?" she said, almost yelling.

Ryōji inched his way toward the door.

"I know, sorry," he said, not bothering to turn around.

"It's okay, but still . . ."

At a loss, Ryōji put on his shoes.

"Ryōji . . ."

"So, let's talk after I get back . . . I have to go now."

"Ryōji?"

He closed the flimsy door behind him, cutting her off.

As he made for the station, the air coiled about his entire body with overwhelming force. A single bead of sweat trailed down the middle of his back.

The windows across the street glowed bright orange with the setting sun.

Another summer, he thought, silently begrudging the season as he did every year.

Ryōji took the Jōetsu bullet train to Takasaki. From there it was another hour by local train to his childhood home.

By the time he arrived in Takasaki, his surroundings were steeped in the ultramarine of summer twilight. The station had been much improved since the bullet lines started coming through here. It used to be that from the bare platform, one could see a smattering of old signs running parallel with the tracks, and long nondescript benches fashioned in yellowish-brown lumber. With this image in mind, he only now remembered that Atsuko was from Takasaki—the reason they had become intimate in the first place.

He boarded the train and took his seat. The exhaustion he had been ignoring at last got the best of him. He sighed and looked down. *Even this floor used to be made of wood,* he mused to himself.

It had been four years since he left for Tokyo, four years since he had ridden this train. As a boy, he treasured those rare outings with Machiko on this very train.

The train jerked from side to side with a loud clang.

Oisan was dead. He almost had to convince himself of it. He closed his eyes and nodded off. Resting his head uncomfortably on the aluminum handlebar, he found himself lulled by the rhythm of the tracks and dreamed.

An especially hot day.

Clumps of yellow flowers bloom as far as the eye could see, rippling outward with the wind.

A young woman stands alone in this sea of yellow, smiling at him pleasingly.

He opens his mouth to say something. She turns away, showing her remarkably slender back. At that moment, he feels caught between fear and anxiety.

—*Wait up.*

Ryōji's voice sticks in his throat, replaced by the frustration of not being able to say what he so lucidly thinks.

—*Wait up.*

His body lurches forward, and something hits his head . . .

Ryōji awoke, rubbing the spot where the metal bar had banged his forehead, and looked to his feet. The floor was imbued with the same pale fluorescent light.

"Oisan is dead," he said under his breath.

The reality of it had yet to sink in, though he had been expecting this day to come. He was starting to remember being on this train four years ago, and the tension shocked him like an unexpected touch.

The train jerked heavily again and the conductor's voice crackled throughout the cabin's interior. Upon hearing his stop announced, he hurried out of his seat.

As he approached the house, he spotted a group of men chatting in the darkness near the gateposts. A large funerary lantern hung at the gate. It had yet to be lit and seemed cruelly out of place. In black inked letters against a white background, the lantern read: *Nakata Family*.

As he quickened his step, one of the men raised a hand in recognition.

"Ah, Ryōji."

It was Koido, head of the neighborhood council.

Koido welcomed him with a clasp of the shoulders before he could even open his mouth.

"Hey, Ryōji's here," he shouted to the house.

"Thank you for everything," said Ryōji, bowing his head in gratitude.

Koido shook his head and urged him inside.

With such a large crowd of people, it was a tight squeeze in an already modest house. As if only noticing it now, Ryōji recalled all the trucks and station wagons parked out front.

He went inside, able only to stand absentmindedly among the throng milling about the living room. He felt a tap on the shoulder.

"Ryōji."

It was Ikuo, his classmate from elementary through high school.

"Ah . . . Ikuo," he said, almost mumbling. Only then did he put down his bags.

Ikuo was the son of a package store owner who ran a shop in front of the station. He and Ryōji used to swim together as children. They hadn't seen each other since high school.

"Welcome back," said Ikuo, who seemed taller.

"Thanks," Ryōji responded, feeling as if the voice were not his own.

"Must be hard for you."

"Yeah. I can't thank you enough."

"About the wake, it's tomorrow night. The funeral will be held the following day."

"Okay."

Ikuo took the bags at Ryōji's feet and disappeared into the inner room. Ryōji followed.

"And Machiko?"

After a moment's pause, Ikuo turned his head back.

"She's inside, but . . ."

The house consisted of a living room, a large sitting room that doubled as the master bedroom, and a smaller room that had once been Ryōji's. The paper doors separating the living room and sitting room were already detached, and an altar was being set up in the former. Which meant she could only be in Ryōji's old room.

"Right," he said, and went in.

Machiko sat alone in the middle of the room, staring into space.

She was dressed in black a day ahead of time, though at least she recognized that Oisan was dead, even if she was frightened of all the strangers making a ruckus in her house.

Upon seeing Ryōji enter, her smile flickered like a fluorescent light.

"Ah, you've come back. My little Ryōji has come back," she said, her face a mixture of confusion, sadness, and a modicum of relief.

"I have."

With that, he sat cross-legged on the floor mat. The room hadn't changed much these past four years.

Once Ikuo set down his luggage in a corner of the room, Ryōji turned to him. Ikuo looked indecisive.

"Did she . . . put these on herself?" Ryōji asked.

"Hm?" Ikuo glanced back at Ryōji, then at Machiko. "Oh, the funeral clothes," he muttered, inclining his head. "Well . . . I'm not sure. Looks that way, doesn't it?"

Ryōji eyed Machiko again.

Her body was so frail, she looked as if she might break from a light squeeze.

She appeared cold and stiff in her black clothing, but her un-made-up profile was strangely beautiful to him. Not surprising, seeing as she wasn't yet forty.

"It's been a long time, hasn't it Ryōji? Where've you been all this time? By the way, Ryōji, have you heard? Oisan is dead. Oh, I guess that's why you came back . . . because Oisan is dead. I'm scared, Ryōji." It was as if she were spouting off in one breath all the things she had been harboring inside until now. He was sure no one had taken the time to listen.

"Yes, I know."

He stared at the floor, nodding to her every word.

"Well, I . . ." said Ikuo softly, leaving the room.

Machiko babbled on. In her gush of words, she kept repeating the same thing: "Where've you been all this time?"

Ryōji thought of all those days he dreamed of coming home, pulled by some unseen chain. And it wasn't just a *desire* to come home. He felt it in his body before it even manifested itself in words. It was an *instinct*.

"Ryōji?" she said, shaking his shoulders.

"Yeah, I know."

He continued staring at the floor mat, thinking of the many years spent living together with Machiko and his father.

Ryōji never knew his birth mother.

Though his father amassed quite a fortune as a stockbroker during the postwar economic boom, Ryōji had almost no memories of that time. From the few snippets gleaned from his father's recollections, he could only imagine his father in his prime holding on to his elusive ambitions and slipping through the cracks of Japan's upheaval to make a name for himself.

During the oil crisis, Ryōji's father had brought him here, the town where he himself had been born. After hitting rock bottom, his father arrived at the station with only a duffle bag in one hand and Ryōji in the other, nothing else to call his own. Ryōji wasn't yet in first grade. His parents were already divorced.

His grandfather had just died. His father lived off the funds he made by selling the land left to him piece by piece. Nearing fifty, his father had exhausted the energy of his youth. Ryōji thought his life had waxed and waned in concert with Japan's rapid growth and decline.

It was then that his father began sleeping around with random women, if only to fill the void of his newfound emptiness.

He had a vague recollection of the women before Machiko. Looking back on it now, he saw no reason they should have been attracted to a washed out fifty-something with no money or regular source of income. Then again, it was quite possible that he simply knew how to win them over. In fact, Ryōji remembered a scene he witnessed when he was little: a woman with dyed hair and a blue sleeveless dress sat stretching her legs out on the floor mat, his father clutching a small bottle in his hand while studying the woman's toenails. Ryōji was too young to realize he was giving the woman a pedicure.

He felt ambivalent about his father, but could easily imagine how such kindness looked to those women. That kindness showed itself in strange ways.

Perhaps this was the source of his father's appeal. Exhausting everything he had, it was the only thing that made him live. Dalliances with women were his way of holding on to something.

Either way, the women he brought home were all very kind to Ryōji. He never had a problem with any of them.

Fished from the depths of the local red-light district, they looked as if they had given up something, and before Machiko his father never stayed with any of them for too long. Those who did try to get to know him better invariably faded from his life once they saw he had nothing to offer.

And yet, the mere prospect of being deprived of their attentions left Ryōji with a profound loneliness. It was then that those little pomegranate seeds began to fill his body with imprisoned emotions.

Machiko entered his life in the summer following his first year of elementary school.

It was an especially hot day. Being a small country town, the school was a forty-minute walk away. When Ryōji came home from his long trek, dripping with sweat, he saw a woman admiring the profusion of flowering weeds in the front yard.

Upon noticing him, she smiled, her face vibrant like the yellow blooms around her.

—*Hello.*

Somehow, Ryōji knew she was next. The mere possibility filled him with joy.

The woman was young and beautiful. What separated her the most from all the others, however, was a certain air of innate purity in the fragility that pervaded her entire being. It was almost as if he could see right through her body.

Most of his father's trysts up to that point had been with prostitutes or women not far from them. Machiko was just twenty or so, and Ryōji learned that she worked as a hairdresser near the next station.

From the first day Machiko came to the house, she called his father "Oisan," even in front of Ryōji. She had meant to call him "Oji-san," an affectionate term for an older man, but her characteristic lisp made it come out as "Oisan."

From the way she spoke, he knew she wasn't from the area. Machiko didn't use the local vernacular. Her manner of speaking had more of a Tokyo flavor to it.

Just when they thought she would use more polite speech, out of nowhere she would come out with some surprisingly vulgar words. Her dialect made it even clearer that she hadn't been raised properly.

Machiko, he heard, was an orphan, passed around from one relative to another until, after graduating from middle school, she started working as a live-in at a hairdresser in Tokyo. Whether she had run away from home or had been kicked out wasn't clear.

After sharpening her skills, she drifted from place to place, living on her own. She never said how she ended up in this area, but in any event she met his father in the neighboring town.

Machiko never had anyone to teach her "common sense" or how to speak properly. Movies and television had been her textbooks.

It wasn't until Ryōji grew older that he began to acquire bits and pieces of her background and began to understand why she had that tinge of aloofness, why she wasn't quite "all there."

Before long, Machiko vacated her apartment and came to live with the two of them. Nothing could have pleased Ryōji more, and this dramatic change practically tickled him with joy. After so many women coming and going, Machiko would be the one to stay.

From then on, he started calling his father "Oisan" as well.

Even in his young heart, he knew this arrangement would have seemed most odd to an outsider. Calling his father "Oisan" in imitation of Machiko was perhaps a way of softening the peculiarity of their relationship. Ryōji was fond of Machiko. He never wanted to her to leave like the others. He fawned himself upon her like a puppy. He and Machiko were equals, and calling his father "Oisan" was a way of maintaining that balance.

He was unsure about that now. He was only a boy then. It therefore never occurred to him that Oisan might not be able to kick his old habits so easily.

And then, something happened. Something that Machiko, and perhaps not even Oisan, could have foreseen: he needed other women even after getting this most beautiful girl, young enough to be his daughter. After only a few years of living together, Oisan's "unfortunate illness" came out of remission.

Still in elementary school at the time, Ryōji couldn't have known why his father kept coming home later and later. It was only because of Machiko's gradual change in mood that he noticed it at all.

Oisan was never good at telling lies. He was better off not telling them at all. The more outrageous the lie, the more desolate the listener felt.

He would come home smelling of perfume, looking for all like a man reborn. But Machiko never faulted him for these indiscretions. Not that she could have gotten a word in edgewise, for whenever Oisan did get back, he would devise the usual excuse and blurt it out before she even had a chance to open her mouth.

Try as he might, Ryōji just couldn't understand his father's addiction. He could only imagine what Machiko must have felt as she sat there taking his blathering excuses, knowing deep down that every word was a lie. The sadness of it all pressed his heart like an iron.

Only now did he understand what his father meant to a loner like Machiko: Oisan had become her haven. That he was old enough to be her father and was a parent himself were trifling matters to her. Though she was just a girl, barely over twenty, it was precisely this dynamic that compelled Machiko to throw herself at his feet.

She was still rather young and utterly beautiful. Had she wanted to, she could have abandoned this unceasingly fickle man and make something of herself.

So why didn't she do that when she had the chance?

Ryōji believed it was because she finally found solace for the first time in her life and was afraid to give it up. To anyone else, Oisan would have been a rogue, but he gave Machiko just the protection she needed. Which was why she couldn't bear to leave it all behind. She was like a figure standing between two high walls of concrete. These walls were closing in on her ever so slowly, conforming to her body rather than crushing it.

Machiko was back from the hairdresser by the time Ryōji came home from school. They usually ate dinner together without waiting for Oisan. That was when the hard times really began for her. After enduring this routine for a while, Machiko picked up some wool yarn and a knitting book. Unable to read any difficult words, she often slid open the door to Ryōji's room and poked her head in, asking in a half-whisper:

—*Ryōji, could you tell me what this says?*

He was only in elementary school at the time. Rubbing the sleep out of his eyes, he grabbed a dictionary and headed for the living room in his pajamas. Under the muddy fluorescent light, he sat hugging his knees next to Machiko until she understood the instructions as written. Machiko hardly ever got upset over anything else, but on these nights she squinted her eyes and clicked her tongue quietly, sometimes whining and unraveling her mistakes.

At such times, he saw her as if through a veil of fever. He was uncomfortable sitting near her as frightening idiosyncrasies worked their way under his skin. Still, he couldn't bring himself to say goodnight and leave her there to grapple with her needles. It was then that he would think back to that summer's day when they first met, the way she smiled like the flowers around her. He felt miserable in front of this woman as she tended to her knitting with such fervor that she might burst into flame at any moment.

And just when he felt himself fading, he heard the clatter of the front door announcing Oisan's return. At this, Machiko sprang to her feet like some wind-up toy and ran to the entrance. It had taken Machiko nearly a month just to learn how to knit a stockinette.

Ryōji would never forget what happened on one such night.

He was in fifth grade. The days were getting hotter, and they closed only the screen doors. After dinner, he was watching TV. She joined him for a while, but soon he was nodding off. Machiko already had her knitting in hand.

She went on knitting, though summer was just around the corner. She had been knitting night after night for some time now, never producing a single sweater or scarf because she would always unravel what she made and start all over again.

Ryōji laid down on the futon in his bedroom. Machiko mumbled to herself in annoyance late into the night in the living room. This was normal for her, so Ryōji thought nothing of it. He turned over to sleep, thinking to himself, *I wish Oisan would just hurry up and come home already . . .*

—*Oh, no!*

The voice was so loud it woke him up.

He looked at the clock. It was just past five in the morning. With daybreak soon approaching, the sky was still steeped with the night's deep blue outside the ground glass window.

—*Oh, no!*

Only half awake, Ryōji thought he was just hearing things and pulled the blanket up over his nose. He heard the voice again, this time with more force.

—*Oh, no! Oh, no! Oh, no!*

Ryōji sat up sluggishly in bed and rubbed his eyes. He opened the sliding door and found that the lights were still on in the living room.

Still groggy, he dragged himself out of bed and went to see what the commotion was about.

Machiko was sitting at the low dining table in the same position he had left her. Upon noticing him, she turned around with a start and flashed him an awkward smile. It was far from the smile he encountered when they first met, now twisted and disturbing. Her complexion was discolored and lined with dried tears and mucus.

Oisan wasn't yet home, though it wasn't his first time being out this late.

Looking for all like a child caught misbehaving, Machiko hurriedly rolled up what was on her knees and tried to hide it, despite not being anything to warrant such discretion.

And then he saw it: a long, knitted cloth that was a foot wide and easily six feet long. It looked like a monster's tongue, and because she kept on knitting from whatever was on hand, it comprised a hideous mishmash of colors. It made him sick just looking at it.

He felt afraid and could only stand there with his eyes wide open, looking back and forth between Machiko's face and the horrid fruit of her labor.

She hung her head, saying timidly:

—*I've run out of yarn . . .*

After knitting all night without pause, she was spent. The skin on the back of her neck looked especially wan under the stagnant fluorescent light.

Despite his youth, he knew something was seriously wrong.

This proved to be a sign of things to come.

When Ryōji hurried home from school later that same day, Machiko was napping in the master bedroom, looking as if she were dead, while Oisan fanned himself in the living room, eyes glued to a ballgame.

Ryōji tried explaining to Oisan what had happened that morning, but Oisan didn't take him seriously. Thinking his father might understand if he saw it for himself, Ryōji went looking for the "monster tongue," but Machiko had stowed it where it couldn't be found.

Hearing that his son was rummaging around in the bureau, Oisan called to him.

—*Hey, Ryōji, what're you doing in there?*

Driven by senseless anxiety, he felt like clinging to Oisan's robe and sobbing like a child half his age.

Not long after, Machiko stopped working, saying she preferred to stay at home. She also gave up knitting, effectively putting a stop to her nocturnal episodes.

Ryōji knew she had given up something. Not that she *needed* to suppress any part of herself for Oisan's sake. She simply knew no other way.

To this day, he believed in a different outcome, if only she had kept her "self" alive.

But all of this was lost on him at the time.

Ryōji ascended the metal steps and opened the frail door to reveal a slender back.

Totally shocked by the sight, he stumbled inside, too impatient to take off his shoes, and grabbed Atsuko by the shoulders.

—*What's wrong?*

Atsuko awoke from her nap by the space heater and looked up at him in surprise.

—*Never mind, it's nothing.*

He squatted down next to her, trying desperately to still his pounding heart.

Atsuko stared at him for a while in silence, before speaking in her careless tone.

—*"It's nothing"? You always say that.*

—*What?*

—*Are you a man or a mouse?*

I guess that makes me a mouse, then, he thought.

"Hey, Ryōji."

He turned around to find Ikuo propped in the doorway.

The same flowers that once gave Machiko that fateful glow bloomed more wildly than ever in the front yard. Ryōji pulled himself together after realizing he had been thinking about his conversation with Atsuko, staring at those flowers the entire time. It somehow felt inappropriate to him.

"Are you alright?" said Ikuo worriedly, taking his hand from the doorframe.

Ryōji felt sure that Ikuo had grown taller.

"Yeah, I'm fine."

"Must be quite a shock for this to have happened so suddenly."

"Well, it was only a matter of time before . . ."

Ikuo located a pair of sandals and stepped down into the yard. Ever since Oisan had fallen ill, there was no one to tend to the flowers, now littered with pieces of flowerpots and a broken watering can.

Oisan suffered his first heart attack one year after Ryōji left for Tokyo. The attack had severely weakened an already poor heart. The doctor told him to be prepared for another, which came about a month ago. Oisan called Ryōji personally to tell him that he had had another spell, and that was the last time Ryōji ever heard his voice.

Every time he heard of his father's condition, one of those seeds inside him let out a scream. Even before having any conscious desire to go back home, he felt his entire being pulled to this town, to this very house, by an inexplicable power.

In the end, however, he never went back. Not until today.

Ikuo stood beside him. He opened his mouth to speak, but thought better of it.

"Ikuo, you've gotten taller, haven't you?"

At this, Ikuo looked at him confusedly and shook his head in silence. Then, in a low voice, muttered, "What are you talking about, Ryōji?"

Veiled in darkness, the yellow flowers swayed in a cool breeze. There were still several people milling about the living room. With Koido in charge, there wasn't much left for Ryōji to do. Even so, he felt guilty just standing there. Ikuo interrupted him as he headed inside.

"Ryōji."

"Hm?"

Ikuo was staring at the flowers.

"Yes?" Ryōji repeated.

Ikuo spoke, his back still to him.

"Don't think so badly of your father."

"What?"

"I was little, too, and I didn't know him all that well."

To this, Ryōji had no response.

"But I did hear about him from my father, who used to see him when he was delivering sake to bars downtown. Sure, your father was a womanizer, but . . ."

At length, he turned around and looked directly at Ryōji. These were hard things for him to say.

"But he was never too modest when it came to Machiko. My father says that even with the ladies at the bars, it was always Machiko this and Machiko that."

Just then, Ikuo's father called to him from inside.

"Uh . . . well, see you tomorrow."

With that, Ikuo ducked inside. Ryōji's mind was more focused on the sound of the wind blowing through the grass.

"Oh," he muttered without thinking, only now realizing why Ikuo looked taller.

Ikuo stood upright, casting a harmonious shadow onto the garden. His posture exuded sheer confidence and spoke of a man who wasn't afraid to think, feel, or say what he felt. Even when a nearly instinctive emotion took over his consciousness, his body would sturdily bear it.

For a while, Ryōji didn't move. The wind blew again, rustling the plants and prompting him to wander slowly back inside.

Around the time Machiko was retreating into herself, Oisan started working, by Koido's intervention, as a guard at a newly built supermarket.

Since leaving the hairdresser, Machiko hadn't stepped foot out-side the house more than necessary, but Oisan didn't seem to care either way. As if starting up a new job gave him the perfect excuse, he fell right back into his old groove, coming home around three or four in the morning, despite getting off at seven.

Machiko turned her attentions to domestic duties. Day after day, she scoured the house from top to bottom on her hands and knees, going so far as to clean the concrete floor in the kitchen with polishing sand. And when she washed Oisan's dress shirts, she starched and ironed them stiffer than any professional might have done.

Watching Machiko scrubbing every corner of the house with her skirt hiked up, ironing with a most devoted air and uncaring of the sweat streaming down her face, made Ryōji think of words like "obstinacy" and "obsession." She was consumed with making Oisan's house perfect.

Perhaps it was a way of testing her self-worth. And yet, to him, all those things she did to confirm what she didn't really want to confirm were like bets one could never win.

In those days, Machiko often told Ryōji as he left for school to bring her back some origami paper and coloring books. Even after all the immaculate housework, she was still left with a good amount of time to kill and needed something to occupy her mind.

Machiko even started cutting Ryōji's hair with the scissors she kept from work, using even the slightest change in length as an excuse to keep up this newfound ritual.

—*There's something forlorn about our hair, isn't there, Ryōji*, she used to say as she stood on her knees behind him. *On someone's head, we caress it—say it's beautiful, even. But once that hair is cut off and falls to the ground, it becomes dirty to us somehow . . .*

This went on for a while.

As she continued cleaning the house, folding paper cranes, and cutting Ryōji's hair, something accumulated like stalagmites inside her. But she never revealed her anger over Oisan's protracted absence, and she continued to perfect her chores. When Ryōji started middle school, he spent less time at home and could never have imagined those things growing inside her would burst forth like a broken dam.

It happened on an early summer's day during his second year.

After every nook and cranny had been cleaned, laundry was done, and dinner was prepared, Machiko would usually absorb herself in her crafts. When Ryōji returned home, she would at least smile and ask him about his day, or talk about the how the dog at Mr. So-and-So's house out back just had puppies.

But on this occasion, Ryōji opened the door with a clatter to a silent house.

Having finished his extracurricular activities for the day, it was six o'clock by the time he got home. Though it was already dark outside, there were no lights on in the living room or the kitchen. But he knew Machiko couldn't have gone out.

Thinking it suspicious, he peeked inside the living room, right behind the front door, only to find her hunched over the coffee table. For a moment, she looked to be asleep, but when he turned on the light, it was clear she wasn't.

Amazingly enough, she was doing origami in the dark, her face almost touching the table.

—*What are you doing?*

He suddenly remembered the knitting incident, and it filled his head with foreboding. Machiko gently lifted her face, glowing in a way he hadn't seen in all those years.

—*Look how small I made it, Ryōji,* she said in her high-pitched voice.

She held out her palm, cradling a tiny red speck.

—*What is it?*

He bent over and brought his face closer, holding his breath.

The speck turned out to be a miniature folded paper crane, about the size of a pinky nail.

He scooted in front of her and seized her. Machiko's shoulders were so delicate, it was as if they might melt away like snow in his grasp.

—*What are you doing?! What have you been doing all day?!*

Ryōji shook her violently back and forth. The red paper crane dropped to the floor from her open hand.

She gave no response. He shook her even more vigorously, calling out her name repeatedly. Without warning, she stood up and brushed him off with such force he wondered where she hid it in such a frail body.

He fell on his bottom, planted to the floor mat.

—*Machiko . . .?*

He looked up at her in shock. She didn't even acknowledge him. She flung open the door into the kitchen.

—*You haven't eaten yet, have you?* she shouted.

He sat there agape, unable to shape his words, and before long heard water flowing in the kitchen sink as she began preparing dinner. He stared at the little red crane next to him, dumbfounded.

Machiko called him for dinner ten minutes later, followed by restless footsteps into the living room as she laid out dinnerware on the table. Ryōji immediately got up and threw himself at her feet.

—*Machiko, please.*

When finished, she had made three settings of plates, chopsticks, and rice bowls. She ignored the boy clinging to her ankles and returned to the kitchen to fetch the teapot before plopping down on the floor mat.

—*Machiko?*

Ryōji sat facing her with his mouth half open as she began shoveling down rice. He watched as she glanced at him from behind her rice bowl.

—*Hurry up and eat.*

At those words, he timidly picked up his chopsticks, gritting against the cold sweat clinging to his body. There was nothing else he could do. He began eating his rice.

A while later, Machiko stood up abruptly. Ryōji drew back in surprise and put his hands on the floor mat, looking up at her. Her body blocked the fluorescent light, casting her face in shadow.

She was looking past him.

When he turned around, he saw through the screen door two brown puppies in front of the garden, their tails wagging. He recalled her story about the neighbor's dog.

Out here in the countryside, dogs and cats were left to wander onto each other's property, and no one raised an eyebrow over it. Machiko cherished the puppies, and most likely had been giving them leftovers whenever they came by. The puppies whined when they saw her get up, wagging their tails excitedly.

She took the one plate she had prepared for Oisan from the table, shuffled hurriedly to the deck, and jerked open the door with a bang. She hurled the plate into the night air, grilled mackerel and all. It shattered into little pieces on the stepping-stone and the fish landed with a splat. The puppies yelped and ran away.

But she wasn't finished. Oisan's rice, miso soup, cold tofu . . . one after another his dishes disappeared from the table, flying from her hands into the garden. Ryōji tried to hold her back, but was again surprised by her strength. He heard her mutter ever so softly:

—*Take this, and this, take it all . . .*

The cicadas outside started their preemptive song.

Another summer, Ryōji thought to himself as he wrapped his arms around his father's raging mistress. A single bead of sweat trailed down his forehead. Her back was also perspiring slightly.

Her frailty became a pain in his heart. Before he knew it, he was crying. Whether from the sweat in his eyes or from sadness, he didn't know.

At long last, she calmed down. He put her to bed and waited in the living room for Oisan to come home in the wake of this taxing ordeal. He had a lot to tell him.

Midnight came, but still no Oisan.

Ryōji eventually dozed off. He heard sounds in his dreams. Even in his sleep, he tried his best to put up with the disheartening loneliness spreading through his toes and creeping up to his throat.

When next he opened his eyes, it was almost dawn. He awoke with a start and hastened to the corridor. Oisan's shoes were still nowhere to be found. Ryōji opened the sliding door to the master bedroom. He stood there petrified, his scream lodging itself in his throat.

Beyond the door on the futon, there was a slender back. It was Machiko's, covered in a robe patterned with morning glories and slumped forward in an unnatural position. She was completely still.

Gripped in her right hand, laid out like a crushed frog, was one of her razors. Her left hand was concealed under her summer quilt, where the sheets were stained red. That pale light unique to daybreak pierced through the sliding door, casting long, thin patterns on a sheet of crimson.

Machiko was rushed to the hospital. Though she regained consciousness a day later, she was never herself again.

At first, she couldn't even say her own name. Oisan nursed her and never left her side. A week later, she could finally say her name but no more.

Against everyone's wishes, Oisan took her back home. Though she didn't refuse the gesture, neither did she seem to remember who Oisan was.

Oisan quit his job. Thanks to Koido again, he found work addressing and folding brochures from home, which allowed him to tend to Machiko all day. Even so, it took six months for her to call him and Ryōji by name, and a full year until she could carry anything even resembling a conversation.

Seeing the way Oisan stayed at her side as if she had just given birth to his firstborn child, Ryōji wondered why he hadn't been like this from the beginning. What he felt for his father was nothing short of resentment.

—*Why?* Ryōji asked, looking at Oisan. *Why didn't you treat her like this before all this happened?*

Oisan smiled faintly.

—*That wouldn't have been possible.*

Ryōji didn't understand it at all.

From then on, he spoke with Oisan no more than he had to. It was the only way he could deal with his own feelings.

—*Are you angry at me?*

His father asked this only once. Ryōji was in high school now, and a hot, humid summer's day found them sitting together in the living room eating cold soba noodles.

He shook his head in silence.

—*I wouldn't blame you for hating me*, said Oisan softly, looking through the window.

The cicadas were in full chorus outside. A bead of sweat was forming on the tip of his nose.

—*I'm done*, he said, putting down his chopsticks.

Slipping on a pair of sandals from the deck, he went down into the front yard to Machiko's flower garden. Oisan watered the flowers in his pajamas, which were vertically striped with white and pale green. Machiko had bought them for him when she and Ryōji left for Takasaki.

Seeing his father hunched over in his faded, worn-out pajamas, Ryōji recalled vividly the morning glory pattern splashed across Machiko's back. Something he had never felt before spiraled inside him with intense heat.

—*I wouldn't blame you for hating me . . .*

Oisan's voice echoed in his ears.

If only he *could* hate him, then it wouldn't be so hard.

But he couldn't. Looking at his weary father, Ryōji loved him so much that he wanted to run up and hug him.

His body was filled with pomegranate seeds. Each contained an inescapable feeling of love. Invisible strings came out of those seeds. If left alone, they would tie him up from the inside.

—*I can't breathe. I'm suffocating.*

He murmured this softly, watching Oisan's aging back as he was watering the flowers.

I'm better off without them, he thought.

If he didn't do anything about these overwhelming feelings, they would swell until there was no room left inside, not even for himself.

Machiko was lying down on the futon, muttering about something. Oisan dropped the watering can and ran up to the deck.

Ryōji told himself that he had had enough. Those lumps of pomegranate seeds didn't know words. He couldn't stop the feelings once they started. They were infringing him.

He heard Machiko's whiny voice coming from the bedroom. Oisan answered her gently, as if soothing a small child.

As he listened to their voices, tears suddenly started streaming from Ryōji's eyes. It drove a stake through his heart, overwhelming with a feeling he had never been able to shake since.

Oisan patted Machiko on the back to quell a coughing fit, but Ryōji knew he never saw her back for what it was.

That day when he saw Machiko slumped over in the dawn, it was as if her back was saying to him, "My body can't endure this anymore." At that moment, the red stains in the sheets seemed to him less like blood and more like the innards of her own pomegranate seeds that had reached the end of their capacity and burst open from inside her.

Ryōji slurped his remaining soba noodles, now salty from his tears and the drivel from his nose. But he finished them all the same.

The cicadas suddenly stopped outside, and the sounds of wind chimes mingled with Machiko's voice in his ears.

Ryōji graduated from high school not long after and relocated to Tokyo.

On the day of his departure, Oisan and Machiko saw him off at the ticket gate. From the way Machiko kept smiling and waving to him, it was clear she didn't know what "leaving for Tokyo" meant.

Oisan hardly uttered a word.

"Take care" was all he said as his son passed through the ticket gate.

Ryōji was overcome with a desire to turn around at that moment, but forced himself forward, one step at a time, without looking back. As he stared at the wooden floor on the train to Takasaki, he kept repeating one thing to himself, burying it deep in his heart:

—*I'll only take care of myself from now on.*

If he felt moved by or attracted by something, he pretended not to notice it. As long as he could survive like this, it would be more than enough.

He was gripped by a feeling that he would never get away from life.

He lived in Tokyo for four years, all the while shutting out that need to go back home in much the same way he resisted the urge to look back at his father when he left.

And just like that, he stopped loving for the longest time.

"Hey, it's time," said Ikuo, opening the sliding door a crack.

Ryōji was sitting cross-legged in front of Machiko, staring blankly as she played cat's cradle.

"Sure, okay."

Though Ryōji was the chief mourner, he really hadn't done much of anything. The wake was about to start.

He urged Machiko to her feet, but she was too involved with her string games to walk, so he carefully removed the tangle from her fingers.

"You should put this away," he said like a kindergarten teacher to one of his students.

Machiko responded with a *humph* before making her way briskly into the living room.

"Everything all right, Ryōji?" said Ikuo over his shoulder. He sounded genuinely worried.

"Fine."

Ryōji suddenly thought, *What a good guy he is*. Images of Ikuo's looming figure from the night before flashed through his mind.

From 6:30 on, people began trickling in to offer incense.

The early summer sunset was late, and there was still light outside. In the oncoming twilight, the large lantern outside glowed so brightly that it looked more festive than funereal.

More people than he was expecting came to offer their condolences. Quite a few he didn't recognize at all. For the first time in a long while, he tried to picture Oisan the way he used to be when he was young, before he came back to the countryside.

Machiko sat beside him, her narrow shoulders wrapped in mourning clothes. Apparently, her tension from the day before was gone, making her look far more collected. Either that, or her anxiety had simply abated to a more tolerable level.

What an unfortunate woman, Ryōji thought to himself as he eyed her with a sideways glance. She was completely oblivious, not even bowing her head to those who came with incense.

In the end, she was never written into the family register. Ryōji thought of the happier times she could have had, and of the many years this little woman in her thirties still had ahead of her. Her body moved languidly as the long line of mourners came to an end. Ryōji was growing tired.

Amid his fatigue, he at first didn't realize what Machiko was trying to do. Those finished with their incense offerings were all talking out front. In the outer corridor, Koido and other funeral helpers were quietly chatting.

Suddenly Machiko stood upright without a sound, inciting a buzz of confusion.

"Machiko?"

Ryōji tried to stop her, but she paid no heed and walked right in front of the altar.

He called out to her again, this time a little louder. He saw that Koido was getting ready to intervene.

She pushed her way through the crowd in the living room and into the master bedroom with such resolution that no one tried to stop her.

Everyone watched her intently. She rummaged inside the master bedroom closet for a while, at last coming back after finding what she was looking for. There was a stir among the crowd.

She held a variegated string of one thousand paper cranes. They spilled luxuriantly from her arms in brilliant contrast to the black of her funeral clothes.

"All this time, folding them," she said, plopping herself down in front of Oisan's photograph at the altar. Ryōji wasn't sure if those words were directed at him or his late father. She might as well have been talking to herself.

Ryōji thought of Machiko folding the tiny crane that day several years ago. She couldn't have been folding cranes all this time with that same sense of dedication. Had she?

Clutching the cranes on her knees, Machiko tilted her head a little.

"Since I was so sick, Oisan was always folding these to speed my recovery."

Hearing that, it made more sense to him now.

Oisan's figure reappeared like a gust of wind blowing into his head. When Machiko was finally able to talk again, he remembered the countless days Oisan spent at her side, and the way she always pestered him to make origami. He could almost hear her voice:

—*Make a kite next. And a helmet after that.*

"But then . . . Oisan got sick, right? So I thought to return the favor. I tried to continue where he left off, but Oisan told me not to."

"He said that? Why?" Ryōji couldn't help asking.

Machiko nodded without looking at him.

"'I'll do it. I'll do it to the very end.' That's what he told me."

Ryōji didn't know what to say.

"But Oisan died before he could finish it."

Ryōji could only watch as Machiko placed her string of cranes at the altar in offering.

He found it hard to imagine a bedridden Oisan folding miniature cranes with those rough, clumsy fingers.

"Isn't that right?" Machiko said to Oisan's photograph. She was crying a little. But Ryōji didn't understand what she meant by that.

Taking a cue from Machiko, Ryōji also looked at the ceremonial picture of his father. Only then did it occur to him. He felt the furrow lines disappearing. He used to think that when Oisan started to come home later and later and Machiko was learning to knit, she stayed on because she was afraid of parting with the solace she had finally found, and that she quit her job and stayed home because she had given up on something. But it wasn't like that at all. She hadn't given up. It was the opposite. Machiko loved Oisan, plain and simple. And she couldn't let go of that feeling.

Koido approached her. She relented and returned dutifully to her seat. Ryōji watched in silence.

The cranes were spread out in front of the altar. He glanced vacantly through the open window at the blinding radiance of the big lantern hanging from the gate.

Suddenly, the words Oisan had said so long ago came to mind:

—*That wouldn't have been possible . . .*

Something inside him ached intensely. It was as if the remnants of every crushed seed were crying out from within.

Oisan, too, must have harbored seeds inside him that he couldn't contain. Perhaps he, too, had driven himself mad over incontrollable impulses.

"That wouldn't have been possible, huh?" he muttered quietly.

He felt like those words were directed at him, but couldn't say why.

Lightning Source UK Ltd.
Milton Keynes UK
UKHW010620140420
361667UK00011B/159

9 781501 749889